Nancy Warren

THE EX FACTOR

HARLEQUIN®

TORONTO • NEW YORK • LONDON
AMSTERDAM • PARIS • SYDNEY • HAMBURG
STOCKHOLM • ATHENS • TOKYO • MILAN • MADRID
PRAGUE • WARSAW • BUDAPEST • AUCKLAND

Recycling programs
for this product may
not exist in your area.

ISBN-13: 978-0-373-79573-4

THE EX FACTOR

Copyright © 2010 by Nancy Warren

ABOUT THE AUTHOR

USA TODAY bestselling author Nancy Warren lives in the Pacific Northwest, where her hobbies include walking her border collie in the rain and watching classic films. She's the author of more than thirty novels and novellas for Harlequin and has won numerous awards. Visit her Web site at www.nancywarren.net.

Books by Nancy Warren

Don't miss any of our special offers. Write to us at the following address for information on our newest releases.

Harlequin Reader Service
U.S.: 3010 Walden Ave., P.O. Box 1325, Buffalo, NY 14269
Canadian: P.O. Box 609, Fort Erie, Ont. L2A 5X3

To Sharon Kearney,
for too many years of friendship to count.

1

"STACY REALLY WANTS the circus theme," Patricia Grange said, a note of appeal in her voice. It was a tone Karen Petersham knew well—the desperate cry of a woman who has spoiled her baby girl for so long she doesn't know how to stop. As one of the top wedding planners in Philadelphia, Karen got her share of spoiled princesses and their bizarre wedding requests, but this was right up there.

"A circus themed wedding is certainly unusual," Karen said smoothly. "You don't get a lot of them."

"It's because of Cirque du Soleil," Patricia explained, throwing her hands out in a gesture of helplessness.

"Cirque du Soleil?" What on earth could a bunch of acrobatically theatrical circus performers have to do with a wedding?

The mother of the bride nodded. "Hudson took Stacy to see the touring production of *Kooza* for their first date. They think it would be romantic to recreate the circus theme for their wedding."

"Well, I guess we can be happy he didn't take her ice fishing for their first date."

The woman smiled weakly. "I suppose so." She straightened the perfectly straight hem on her Gucci skirt. "Cirque is about both clowning and acrobatics, of course."

"Two excellent attributes of a successful marriage."

"Exactly." The woman smiled at her gratefully. "And Cirque did perform at the Academy Awards one time. I remember seeing it on television."

Only a Philadelphia society girl could equate her wedding with the Academy Awards. Already Karen suspected that this ceremony was going to be one of those nightmares. The mother of the bride had shown up for the appointment, but no bride. Always a bad sign. She was conscious of a wish to tell the woman to take her flying circus acrobats and find another wedding planner, but she didn't. As much as she despaired over some of the demands made of her and her company, If You Can Dream It, Karen also got the most juice out of the toughest assignments. Frankly, the challenges stopped her from succumbing to boredom.

Rich October sunshine streamed through the windows of the renovated brick warehouse she'd bought in Old Town to house her growing business, bringing out the rich caramel in the floors she'd had restored.

"Let me see what I can do. I'll put together a proposal for you and we can meet again, shall we say in two weeks? Perhaps with the bride this time."

When the mother left, Karen sat for a few minutes, typing her notes into her computer, then she got up and walked through the office.

"I'm going to see Chelsea," she said to her assistant, Dee, on the way out. The young blonde British girl who was both support staff and her assistant wedding planner nodded, unsurprised, since Karen took the short walk to her caterer and good friend's premises at least once a day. She trekked to Hammond & Co. to discuss jobs with Chelsea Hammond, her exclusive caterer, or simply to chat with the woman who'd become a close friend. And if she walked the two blocks briskly enough, that was as good as fifteen minutes on the treadmill.

Slipping on sunglasses and a light coat, she strode toward the storefront where Chelsea sold takeout gourmet food and coffee while she ran her growing catering business from the huge industrial kitchen in back. Upstairs was a small apartment that she used as her office.

Chelsea was placing a heaping bowl of quinoa salad into the display case when Karen walked in. She only knew it was quinoa because a sign said so. Unlike her friend, food was not her passion but her enemy and she tried to think about it as little as possible. She certainly wasn't one for cookbooks and those endless TV torture shows featuring gorgeous men preparing mouthwatering meals—two things she most wanted and that were so bad for her, with her figure that was both top-heavy and bottom-heavy on a much too short frame.

The caterer—blessed by nature with a long, slim body that was neither top- nor bottom-heavy, but just right—smiled her rich, slightly mischievous smile at Karen as she straightened from her task. "Perfect, you're just in time for coffee."

"Make mine with cream. And I want one of your four-thousand-calorie brownies to go with it."

Since Karen was on a perpetual diet, Chelsea raised her brows. "Bad day?"

"The bride wants a circus theme. Cirque du Soleil, no less."

Chelsea poured two cups of coffee, deftly popped several decadent treats onto a plate and called out to someone out of sight in the back kitchen, "I'm taking a break upstairs. Keep an eye on the front and call me if you need me."

"'Kay," came the reply.

They hiked up the stairs and Karen said, "I wonder if the wedding night will feature trapezes and human pyramids."

"Your cynicism is showing," Chelsea said, as though it were a slip hanging below her skirt hem.

Karen sighed. "I know. Easy for you, with a big rock sparkling on your finger and the world's cutest guy in love with you, but I'm a bitter divorcee. The wedding planner who doesn't believe in marriage."

"Sure you do," Chelsea soothed. "You simply haven't found the right man."

"I'm thirty-five years old. And the brides get younger every year." She gazed longingly at a brownie. "And thinner. I should give up and let myself get fat. It's not like anyone ever sees me naked. If I'm not getting sex, at least I should take pleasure in food."

"You are not fat, what you are is voluptuous." The woman saw where Karen's eyes were straying and said, "I know you. If you eat that brownie you'll only torture yourself." Her brown eyes twinkled. "But that lemon dream bar is low-cal."

"You're too good to me," she sighed, almost snatching the yellow confection off the plate.

"Are you kidding me? I wouldn't have this great location or half the business I have if it wasn't for you. I am so happy you took a chance on me."

It was true, Karen mused as she bit into a lemon-flavored slice of paradise. When they'd first met,

Chelsea Hammond had just returned from cooking school in Paris and was trying to launch her own catering business. When Karen had tasted the woman's food and chatted with her for a few minutes she'd experienced the gut deep excitement of knowing she'd found the missing piece of her wedding planning business. She'd pretty much signed up Chelsea on the spot to be her exclusive caterer. It meant that no other wedding planner could use the services of Hammond & Co., though she was free to cater any other events on her own. In return, Chelsea got all of If You Can Dream It's catering, and there was a lot of that.

Chelsea opened a computer file on her desktop computer. "When is this wedding circus scheduled?"

"Depends on Cirque du Soleil's schedule."

The woman glanced up, her dark brown hair swinging. "Wow."

"Yeah. Apparently somebody on the groom's side knows somebody who might be able to get them to perform at the wedding." She shook her head at the enormity of the task ahead of her. "We will need a huge space, lots of height. The bride thinks she might want an honest-to-God circus tent."

"I'll play with some ideas for food." Chelsea twisted her mouth to one side. "Not that circus exactly screams matching food. I'll have to work on decoration and presentation." She typed a few more words. "Laurel's the one who'll be thrilled."

Laurel Matthews was a cake maker and decorator of such extraordinary talent that her cakes were true works of art and architecture and, equally amazing, they tasted delicious. An If You Can Dream It wedding was notable for meticulous planning, delicious food, and a cake that always surprised and delighted. "You're right. She'll love the challenge. I can't even imagine what she'll dream up," Karen said.

"Which is what's so great about her cakes."

"I've got another prospect coming this morning— she's looking for a May or June wedding next year, is that a problem for you?"

Chelsea glanced up, looking slightly puzzled. "No, why would it be?"

Karen had been trying delicately to find out when this woman who was engaged to the man of her dreams was actually getting married. So far, subtle hadn't worked. "I'm wondering when you and David are getting married. Won't you need some time off?"

Chelsea waved a hand, her engagement ring catching the light and sending out a spray of fireworks. "Don't worry. We'll get around to it. We're just both so busy right now."

"That man needs to stop playing hard to get," she snapped.

Karen still hadn't entirely forgiven David Wolfe for making a deal with Chelsea to pose as his fake fiancée in order for him to snag a promotion at work. Of course he'd fallen in love with Chelsea along the way. Who wouldn't? She was gorgeous, a gourmet cook and one of the sweetest women Karen had ever met. So, had he snapped up this amazing woman when she'd obviously loved him? No, of course not. Being a man, he had no idea when the greatest woman in Philadelphia was right under his nose. Instead, he'd almost lost her.

Karen would never forget the heartbroken woman who had taken refuge in this very space, living in the small suite she now used as her office while she struggled to get her business going and forget David, the man who had broken her heart.

Fortunately, he'd come to his senses just in time and now they were engaged for real, living in his amazing town house in Rittenhouse Square. But Karen would be a lot happier when the engagement ended in marriage.

What was stopping David? Did he really want to lose this woman again?

"He's fine. Really. We're both fine."

She didn't believe it for a minute, but she also knew that Chelsea wasn't one to unburden herself easily. She'd talk to Karen when she was ready.

Deciding she had too much on her plate with circus acts and new business coming in every day to worry about why her best friend wasn't in a hurry to marry the man she was engaged to, she reluctantly drained her coffee cup.

When she returned to her office, Karen felt calmer. The taste of lemon clung to her lips and the idea of a circus for a wedding seemed more ludicrous than annoying.

"The Swensons asked to move their appointment back half an hour," her assistant said. "And two new messages came in. I put them on your desk with your mail."

"Great, thanks."

She stepped into her office. The Hepplewhite desk had nothing on it but her laptop, the big leather-bound day planner she still used in spite of technology, the small stack of mail and the phone messages.

She had ten minutes until her next appointment, a new client, Sophie Vanderhooven, and while she waited she flipped open the newest bridal magazine. It was important to keep up with the latest trends, though after ten years in the business she found trends fairly predictable. Now, for instance, with so much uncertainty in the world, weddings were turning strongly traditional. When the economy boomed and wars were somewhere else, then more couples tended to exchange vows on the beach wearing love beads or shouted their I Do's from hang gliders.

She was skimming an article about nonallergenic bouquets when her assistant beeped her intercom. "Ms. Vanderhooven and her fiancé are here," she said.

"Thanks. I'll be right out."

A quick peek in the mirror she kept in her top drawer confirmed that her mouth was now free of tell-tale lemon dream bar crumbs, her red hair was confined into a smooth bun, her mascara unsmudged. A quick swipe of lip gloss and she stepped back into the towering heels she wore to raise her closer to her dream height of five foot ten from her God-given, stingy five-two.

Her practiced smile on her face, she stepped out to greet her latest clients. She reached the reception area and stalled, her hand already half extended, her mouth open to speak. But nothing came out.

Normally, she gave her initial attention to the bride since she was almost always the true client, while the groom was only peripherally involved. But the man who rose from the plush waiting room seats was not one she could ignore.

He was still commanding, still gorgeous in that careless way of a man who's so used to female attention he barely notices it. Keenly intelligent gray eyes held her gaze, a twinkle of amusement lurking in their depths. His hair was still dark, though a few threads of silver glittered at his temples. Neither of them spoke, then a female voice broke into her trance.

Her hand was taken in a cool clasp. "Hello. I'm

Sophie Vanderhooven, I'm so pleased to meet you. And this is Dexter Crane."

Automatically, Karen pumped her hand up and down, forced her mouth back into some semblance of normality. "Nice to meet you."

She inclined her head at the man still staring at her. "Mr. Crane." There was a slight pause as the three of them stood there before she pulled herself together. "Um, won't you come into my office?"

She turned and began walking.

She felt his eyes on her all the way, and bitterly did she regret every calorie she'd so foolishly imbibed in the five years since she'd last laid eyes on Dexter Crane. A woman had her pride. The last thing she wanted was to look fat in front of her soon-to-be-married ex-husband.

Especially from behind.

2

"WHEN ARE YOU and MR. Crane planning to be married?" she asked in her most professional tone. She'd taken her place behind her desk and motioned for the happy couple to occupy the two pretty chintz chairs opposite.

A well-bred laugh answered her. A finishing school hah-hah, perfectly-modulated and quiet. "I'm not marrying Dexter. He's the best man, but my fiancé is out of the country and he asked Dex to come along with me so I don't get carried away."

Her gaze rose and connected with Dexter's. Yep, that was definitely a glimmer of amusement. Bastard. He was enjoying this.

"I see." In a much lower voice she muttered, "Lucky escape for you."

"Pardon?"

"I said, 'It's a lucky thing you've come early in the season.' Things really book up. Well, what do you have in mind, Ms. Vanderhooven?"

The young woman's ideas were lifted right out of the

current issues of bridal magazines. Clearly, she'd been perusing every one.

"And I thought maybe I should have a non-allergenic bouquet, you know, in case anyone's allergic." There was a moment's pause. Karen took refuge in taking notes so she could think of the questions that might help her discover what this bride really might like, ideas that wouldn't change every month when a new batch of wedding mags hit the newsstands. Then Sophie said, "But I'm very open to suggestions."

Dexter said, "I'm not the one getting married here, but I've always thought something a little less formal would be nice. A garden wedding, let's say."

Her pen slipped, drawing a squiggly line right through the word *bride*. She realized her hands were sweating, that's why her pen had slipped.

She and Dex had married among a garden of roses and irises, her favorite flower of all, and lilies, so the perfumes intermingled. Even as he spoke the words she was transported back to that magical day, the day she'd thought would begin her own personal happily-ever-after.

Fool.

"I'm sure Ms. Vanderhooven has the best ideas for her own wedding."

"Not really," the bride said. "I'm pretty open to ideas. And Andrew always listens to Dexter, so we thought if he came instead it would be almost as good."

"Dexter, that's an unusual name." Karen frowned. "Makes me think of the serial killer on TV."

Dexter shot her an "oh, come on," look and explained that Dexter was his mother's maiden name, as though she didn't know it perfectly well. Then he rose. "I think better on my feet. You see, Ms. Petersham, mind if I call you Karen? It was Karen, wasn't it?" He didn't wait for an answer, naturally, and continued, "You see, Karen, most people want to feel that a marriage is forever, so you want something that's going to mean something in fifty years. You want a wedding you'll look back on with fond memories."

She felt her color heighten as she locked gazes with him. "Do you?"

KAREN HAD A SPLITTING HEADACHE the rest of the day. She knew it wasn't only the stress of seeing Dex again, but the added insult to her body of skipping lunch. Of course she knew that depriving herself of a few calories wouldn't suddenly make her magically thin or grow her half a foot so she could look Ms. Sophie Vanderhooven in the eye—and spit in Dexter's. She'd skipped lunch anyway, which she knew wasn't good for her, all the diet books said so, but sometimes she refused to believe their logic.

And ended up with a headache as well as a cranky, empty stomach.

With no further appointments, she settled in to work on her monthly accounts, not that there was much point in it since she couldn't concentrate. All she could do was relive that moment when Dexter had walked back into her life. Worse, it was clear that he, Sophie and the missing groom had all agreed to appoint him stand-in groom and assistant wedding planner, which had her hauling the large bottle of painkillers out of her emergency drawer and swallowing two of them with the zero calorie water on her desk.

Dee popped her head in the door at a few minutes before five and said, "Is it okay if I head out now?" She grinned. "I've got to get home and change for my date tonight."

Sure, Dee was thin, gorgeous, young and had that British accent going for her, but she seemed to get more than her fair share of dates.

"Where do you meet all these men?"

"Online," the younger woman said, her blue eyes twinkling with excitement. "It's mad fun, you should try it."

"Online dating? It seems so desperate."

"It's not. I do it all the time." Dee didn't bother saying she wasn't desperate. All you had to do was look at her. "Our trouble is that we work in an industry that caters to women, and the only men who come round here are already spoken for. Honestly, you should at least give it a go."

"I don't know."

"Tell you what, I'll set you up a profile tomorrow and show you how to get on. It's really simple and gives you a chance to screen someone first before you waste your time meeting them."

"I guess I should be open-minded," Karen said. Normally she'd have scoffed, but seeing Dexter today was making her feel more than usually single. And vaguely desperate.

"You'll have fun, I promise."

A slight woman with multicolored hair that looked as though Edward Scissorhands was her hairdresser drifted in behind Dee. She blinked big eyes and glanced around as though wondering where she was and what she was doing here.

"Hi, Laurel," Dee said.

"Hello."

"What do you think about Plenty of Phillys?"

"The online dating site?"

"That's right."

Laurel pulled her sketchbook out of her peace-sign-emblazoned bag. "I don't think about it. Why?"

"Honestly, Laurel, how do you manage in the real world? I don't mean do you contemplate the site the way you'd meditate on world peace or whatever you do when you sit around cross-legged and chant aum, I mean what do you think about Karen doing the online dating thing?"

"Oh." The cake decorator turned her huge eyes to Karen. "Do you want to meet men on the Internet?"

"Of course she does, she's desperate," Dee announced. "And you should try it, too." She sent them both a megawatt smile. "Right, then, see you tomorrow."

"Yes. Have fun tonight."

Once Dee had gone, Karen turned to Laurel. "I'm not definitely going to do it, I'm only thinking about it."

"I think you should do whatever makes you happy."

And the amazing thing about Laurel was that when she said wacky things like that, she actually meant them. "I know you do. So, what have you got for me?"

Laurel was in the habit of bringing in her cake designs for Karen to approve. Not that she needed to, everything she baked was incredible, but Karen suspected she liked the reassurance of her approval.

But she really wished the woman didn't bring sketches of the most delectable treats that looked so good even in the sketchbook that Karen's mouth started to water. Especially not at the end of the day when her willpower was at its lowest ebb.

Once she'd approved half a dozen designs and they'd gone over timing and delivery of the cakes for this weekend, Laurel drifted out of the office and Karen got back to her accounts.

After giving in to her hunger and nuking a Lean Cuisine meal, she continued wrestling with her books for another couple of hours. When the muted chime that announced an after-hours caller rang, she wasn't surprised. She supposed on some level she'd expected him.

Ignore the bell or go answer him?

It really wasn't an option. With a sigh, she rose and stepped back into her heels and took her time going to the front door.

In the dim light he looked almost a stranger to her, so tall and elegant and, she reminded herself sternly, no longer hers.

"You look good, Kiki."

In spite of herself she smiled. "No one's called me that in years."

"Good."

It was cold outside and she shivered.

"Can I come in?"

Only now did she realize they were both standing at the entrance.

She stepped back to usher him in. "Of course."

Once more he followed her into her office. He glanced around as though he hadn't been there earlier that very day. "Place looks good. You've done well for yourself."

Not compared to him. After they'd split, he'd become one of the top architects in New York, the go-to guy for bringing faded grandeur back from near death. He was fanatical about reclaiming and modernizing heritage properties and designing new buildings or additions to fit the old neighborhoods. She felt his approval at the way she'd used the best of the old building she occupied while still managing to bring in ultramodern conveniences.

"Do you own the building?"

"Not that it's any of your business, but yes I do."

He nodded. "Smart girl."

"Too smart to be charmed by you." She sighed. "What do you want, Dex?"

"I don't know." He scratched his head and her eyes were drawn to the thick, black hair she remembered so well. "I knew this was your outfit, obviously, but I thought it would be fun to surprise you."

"You certainly did surprise me." But if almost giving her a heart attack was supposed to be fun, she thought she'd pass.

His gray all-seeing eyes locked on hers. "You didn't tell Sophie about our past."

"Didn't seem very good for business to bring up my divorce when the woman's here to plan a wedding." She shot him a glance. "Did you tell her?"

"No." He picked up her gold Montblanc pen off the desk, ran his thumbnail over the monogram. "I decided to leave it to you." He'd given her that pen back in happier times, and now she was annoyed with herself for her sentimentality in using the damn thing every day.

"So, we don't tell the lucky couple that their wedding planner and his best man used to be married?"

"No, I guess not."

"And that we hate each other?"

He put down the pen, straightened to his full six feet and looked down at her. "I never hated you. That's your department."

A moment passed and she pressed her lips together to keep from crying out that she missed him. Instead she said, "Why are you here, Dex? I mean, in the city. You work in New York now."

"I do. But I'm quoting on a project here in Philadelphia. A grand old structure that's been a home, a warehouse and a boardinghouse, to name a few." Enthusiasm lit up his eyes. "She's a tired old girl, but with amazing bone structure. The best of the original architectural features are intact and the client wants to work with them, while bringing the building up to date. It's going to be a boutique hotel and retail combination."

"Sounds amazing, and right up your alley."

"It is. I really want this one. And if it works out, you'll be seeing a lot of me."

She raised one eyebrow.

"Helping Sophie and Andrew plan their wedding."

He looked so sincere, so good, so sexy that for a moment she forgot the reason she'd divorced him. The five-foot-ten blonde goddess she'd found half dressed and wrapped around her husband. The saddest aspect of that fiasco was that on some level she'd noted that Dexter and the former model had looked natural together, two tall, glamorous super-people.

"You're good at planning weddings, not so good at staying faithful once you're in one." Her venom seemed to curdle the air.

"Like I said, hate was always your department."

"Well, I got over it." With a lot of tearful sessions with her girlfriends and some rather expensive ones with a therapist. "Now I've accepted that our marriage was a mistake."

"You sure didn't fight for it."

The old, familiar anger began to surge inside her

but she bit her tongue and counted to ten. Then eleven. Finally twelve before she felt calm enough to speak.

"Why would I fight to keep an unfaithful husband?"

He shook his head. "I don't know why I bother, but I am telling you again that I never had sex with that woman. She was drunk and crazy."

"Didn't look like you were trying very hard to peel her off you."

"Believe me, I was, and I could have used your help that night instead of having you turn tail and abandon me."

Oh, how she wished she could believe him, could have believed him six years ago when it had happened. But she didn't believe him, and couldn't imagine living with a man who thought so little of her that he'd betray her like that.

"I guess maybe we were wrong about each other."

"I guess so."

He shoved his hands in his pockets, leaned against her desk, looking ridiculously masculine against the feminine lines of the furniture; it appeared as though the wood might snap from the weight of him leaning on it. But like her, the piece was stronger than it looked. "You're still the sexiest woman I've ever known."

She snorted. "Oh, please."

"Or maybe it was us together. I miss a lot of things about you, but mostly I miss you in my bed." He looked at her with such intensity that she felt her blood begin to pound. Of course she remembered. When she wasn't cursing the man for his faithlessness she spent more time than she should cursing him for giving her the kind of sex that she'd never found before or since. Soul-scorching, sometimes tender, sometimes dirty but always intimate. She was secretly pleased that he hadn't found that again either. Or so he said. But then maybe that was another line in the player's handbook. How would she know?

She forced herself to meet his gaze coolly. Took a deep breath and uttered the biggest lie of her life. "I don't miss you."

She should have recalled that nothing ignited Dexter's competitive instincts like a challenge. She saw heat flash in his eyes, anger and lust and a mix of emotions she couldn't begin to identify.

One second he stood there before her and the next he was pulling her to him, crushing his mouth against hers so fast that she couldn't have moved away if she'd tried. She uttered a muffled protest, squirmed against him and then as the inevitable tide of heat swamped her, found herself melting into that oh, so familiar embrace.

The initial hardness of his kiss softened and he began to play with her, igniting all her responses until she was crazy with pent-up lust and a need so strong she couldn't begin to stifle it. She was so weak-kneed she clung to him, responding wildly, mindlessly.

Every part of her ached and burned and throbbed. If he threw her down on the Hepplewhite desk now, or even on the reclaimed hardwood floor, she'd let him take her and both of them knew it.

Then, as suddenly as he'd moved on her, he let go and stepped back. His breathing was faster than normal, his mouth wet from hers. Still, he managed to sound cool when he said, "I don't think I believe you."

Then he turned and headed for the door. "Don't work too late."

3

"WHAT ABOUT THIS GUY?" Dee asked as they cruised the single man ads on the online dating site that she insisted had the best success with Philly singles. They were in her office and Dee had just finished setting up her account. Even twenty-four hours ago, Karen knew she wouldn't have put up a profile on something called Plenty of Phillys but since that scorching kiss yesterday, she was determined to get out there and try to find a genuine, decent man who wouldn't screw around the second her back was turned. Wouldn't melt her with his kisses when he came back into her life.

But the man whose photo she was looking at on her computer definitely wasn't that guy.

"I want to correct his spelling," she said.

Dee sighed and moved to the next one. Mohawk, tattoos and a spiked dog collar. "Ick," they said in unison.

The third profile featured a perfectly average-looking man with glasses, a full head of hair, and, perhaps more important, a profile written by someone who'd obviously passed high school English. "He's a CPA, never been married, but looking to find a partner." Dee glanced up at her. "That's good, right?"

"Yes." Karen finished reading his profile. "I like that he mentions taking things slow. I really can't handle fast right now."

"Great, let's send him a wink," Dee said pushing a couple of buttons before Karen could slap her hand away.

"What have you done?"

Dee laughed, the happy trill of a woman who dates regularly and isn't scarred by love. Yet. "You have to let them know you're interested. That's how it works. You send a wink."

"I am so not ready for this."

"You so are." Her assistant danced out of the office. "Call me if you need me."

Dee hadn't made it to the door when a funny noise emanating from her laptop made Karen squeak, "I need you."

Dee peeked over her shoulder. "Hey, he winked back."

"Is that good?"

"That's great. Means he read your profile and he's interested. He's online now, so you can chat. Look, he's sent you a message. Click here."

Hello, Karen. I see you are a virgin.

"A virgin?" she squealed. "What is he, a pervert?"

"Would you relax?" her twenty-three-year-old mentor insisted. "Read on. He means you're new to the site."

"Oh. He says, 'here's a bit more about me.' Um, I think he's included his resume."

"Just give the guy a chance. And remember, there

are lots of guys out there, so don't be afraid to keep looking."

"Okay. Thanks."

She kept reading. He had sent her a profile, obviously prewritten for such an occasion and if he hadn't included his resume, there wasn't much about his schooling and work life she didn't know when she'd finished. In the back of her mind she was thinking how much her business could benefit from a decent CPA, then she remembered she was supposed to be looking for romance, not accounting services.

His name was Ron and he did sound like a nice guy. Nothing flashy, which was good. She was pretty sure, for instance, that he wouldn't shove a woman against her own desk and kiss her senseless. Certainly not without first asking permission. Then she was for damn sure that he wouldn't waltz back out of her office, having made the point that she was still desperately attracted to him, and leave her seething with sexual frustration as well as anger at her own stupidity.

Which made Ron a lot closer to perfect than certain men she could name.

She replied to Ron, telling him a bit about herself.

Then she clicked off and got back to work.

When she checked her e-mail again at the end of the day, she had a few random winks, and Ron had replied. She had to admit it was nice to make "get to know you" conversation with a man, even if it was next door to anonymous.

He ended by inviting her for coffee. I always do coffee as a first date, he explained, obviously catering to her "virgin" status. There's no pressure. It's only an hour of our time and if we don't want to continue that's fine. And if we do, then we go from there. What do you think?

What did she think?

She had no idea, so she decided to lay the entire situation before Chelsea.

"Online dating?" her friend said when she'd walked over to her place to ask for advice. "Wow. I've never tried it, but some of my girlfriends met boyfriends and husbands that way." She shrugged. "And a few use the site to find booty calls."

"Booty calls? Seriously?"

"Hey, different strokes."

Karen bit deeply into a lemon dream bar before saying, "Honestly, I don't even know what I'm doing. I think I'm scared."

"Honey, you book acrobats for weddings, you drag grooms to weddings on time, solve blended family conflicts that would baffle the entire Oprah/Dr. Phil team. I once saw you personally climb a tree to fix twinkle lights. While wearing four-inch heels. I think you can handle a cup of coffee with a CPA."

"I guess you're right." She put a hand to her chest where her heart was beating rapidly.

Chelsea looked at her with concern. "You seem way more bent out of shape than seems appropriate for a coffee date. What's going on?"

"Oh, Chelsea, it's all such a mess," she wailed and promptly shoved the last of the lemon dream into her mouth. Once she'd taken what comfort she could from the food, she told her friend everything, from her first meeting Dexter at a party, to their wedding, the marriage, the betrayal, to him coming back into her life. She ended with the kiss.

"Scumbag!" was Chelsea's succinct response to the

story. For which Karen was enormously grateful. "And now he thinks he can waltz into your business and try to get back in your pants? I don't think so."

"Yeah, I know."

"Getting out and dating new men is a fantastic idea. Really. Get your mind off your ex."

"I suppose you're right."

"I am right. And you know what else you need?"

She thought of some of the other well-meaning advice Dee had dispensed from time to time. "Please don't say sex toys."

Chelsea grinned at her. "I am assuming that you have a good selection, as every woman should. But no, I was referring to a girls' night out."

"Oh, I would love that." A night off from worries and stress with some of her female friends would be sooo good.

"Okay." And as she saw Karen's mouth open Chelsea stopped her, saying, "And, Ms. Planner Extraordinaire, this is one that I'll be planning. You come and have a good time. That's all. Got it?"

Impulsively, she hugged her. "Got it. Thanks."

"WE'RE SEAHORSES," the voice on the phone explained.

She really didn't charge enough for this job. "Seahorses? Maybe you need an aquarium, not a wedding planner," Karen said as gently as she could.

The young woman's laugh was sudden and loud in her ear. "No, I mean me and Steve, the guy I'm marrying, we belong to the Seahorses Scuba Diving club."

"Oh, okay, I get you."

"You must have thought I was nuts," the woman said, with another boisterous laugh.

Karen joined in, hahaha, without admitting she'd assumed the woman was certifiable. Or that she wouldn't be the first crazy person who'd hoped If You Can Dream It was a company designed to make any hallucination come true.

"Before I waste both of our time in a meeting, I want to ask you if you could arrange an undersea wedding."

"An undersea wedding, like *The Little Mermaid?*"

"I guess, sort of. See, we dive the wrecks off the Jersey shore and we were thinking it would be so cool to get married underwater."

"Oh, wouldn't it." Karen rubbed her temple. Surely you couldn't get a headache this fast. "Hard to cut the cake, though."

More laughter greeted her. "I can see we're going to get along fine. No, what I'm thinking is if we could rent a glass-bottomed boat for the guests and then me and Steve could get married underneath. We wouldn't have thought of it, but we met a JP who also dives. He could perform the ceremony from the boat, and we'd be wired for sound. Instead of saying, 'I do,' we'd give the thumbs up sign. Isn't that totally cool?"

"Oh, totally."

"We want to get married next August. We need some ideas. We really want our wedding to stand out as something different."

No problem there.

"So, will you do it?"

"Arrange a wedding on a glass-bottomed boat so two scuba divers can give a thumbs-up?" She shook her head. "Sure, why not?"

"Great, when can we come in to see you?"

She made an appointment for the scuba sweethearts,

and then almost broke down and wept when her next appointment informed her that she wanted a completely traditional wedding. Church, flowers, white gown, bridesmaids, hotel reception, everything simple and staid and normal. How refreshing.

As she was finishing up the proposal, Sophie Vanderhooven called sounding excited. "I heard Melissa Stanhope got the most divine cake for her wedding this Saturday."

"Yes, it's lovely. Laurel, our cake maker has a real gift."

"But Cinderella's coach? That is such an amazing idea." She now recalled that it was the Stanhopes who had recommended her services to the Vanderhoovens.

"Even better, the cake is made with pumpkin."

"I know! She told me. Can I have something like that for my wedding?"

"Of course you can." Did this woman not have any original ideas of her own? "Not the same cake, of course, because Laurel creates a unique design for every event, but you can give her guidelines."

A sigh wafted over the phone. "Mother wants a traditional tiered cake complete with little plastic bride and groom on the top, but I want something more romantic, more me."

"I'm sure we can find something that will make you and your mother both happy," she said diplomatically.

"I hope so. Anyhow, I'll see you Saturday."

"Saturday?"

"At Melissa's wedding."

"Oh, of course. Though I'm not a guest. If I do my job right, you shouldn't even notice me."

Sophie laughed in her elegant way. "No one could miss you."

Before she could ask what that was supposed to mean, in a polite way, the woman was gone.

Puzzled, she got up and walked to the front reception area. "Dee?"

Her assistant glanced up from matching the place cards to the Stanhopes' master guest list. "Mmm-hmm?"

"Do I stand out in a crowd?"

Dee blinked at her. "You have Amy Adams's face and hair and Marilyn Monroe's body, and, I don't know, a sort of commanding way about you. It's what makes you a great wedding planner. Everyone scurries when you tell them to. So yes. Of course you're noticeable."

"Huh. Thought I was being so discreet." She wandered back toward her office.

"Hey, speaking of discreet, when are you meeting that CPA?"

"We're having coffee Sunday afternoon."

"Brilliant. I can't wait to hear about it on Monday."

"What's the weather forecast for tomorrow?"

Dee didn't have to look, she'd already checked. "Low fifties, no precipitation expected."

"Wonderful. A perfect day for a late fall wedding."

And so it was, she realized when she rose the next morning. The day was dry, the sun was shining and there was no snow on the ground. After showering and doing her hair in a restrained bun, she slipped into a navy pencil skirt and white blouse, then pushed her feet into her high-heeled navy pumps. Discreet and professional, that's how she thought a wedding planner should look.

Amy Adams indeed. Dee must be angling for a raise.

4

"WE CAN'T FIND the best man," Mr. Stanhope hissed into Karen's ear.

So far, everything for the Stanhope wedding had been going smoother than a chocolate milkshake. This was her first lump. "Has he answered his cell phone?"

"I don't think so."

"I'll get right on it. In the meantime, Mr. Stanhope, remember, you hired me to take care of problems. I'll stall the bridal party." Her calm manner and soothing smile had their desired effect. The father of the bride's high color receded and he nodded, standing straighter in his tux.

"Glad to have you onboard."

"We may need to call in a stand-in, but I promise, you'll have a best man for your daughter's wedding.

"Keep an eye on things out front," she whispered to Dee, then, without any visible haste, she walked from the front of the church and out into the parking lot. Guests were still arriving but the bridal party was scheduled to pull up in fifteen minutes.

She slipped into her car and reached for the Stanhope

wedding binder. In it was all the information she could possibly need, including home and cell numbers for the missing man.

She called both and was invited twice to leave a message. Which she did. Not good.

She then called the driver of the limousine bringing the bridal party to the church and asked him to take a detour. "I need five extra minutes."

"No problem."

Having stalled the bride, she left her car and slipped into the church through a side entrance. She knew her way around most of the churches and synagogues of the city. She made her way to the anteroom where the groom and his party would be waiting.

The groom looked a little pale, but steady. He glanced up when she entered. "I'm going to kill Brian. He promised he'd be here."

"Does he have issues with punctuality?"

"Not usually."

Her cell phone rang. "Ah." Sure enough, it was the best man. "Flat tire," he panted. "I went to change it, but that is my spare."

"Where are you?"

He named a location that was a good five minutes away. "Are you dressed to go?"

"Yep."

"All right. I'll come and get you."

She turned to the groom. "Appoint a stand-in just in case."

"But the ring?"

She slipped a plain gold band from her right hand. "I always carry a spare." Then she smiled at him. "Good luck."

"Thanks."

She sprinted to her car and made her way out of the parking lot, now quieting as most of the guests had arrived. She was in time to see Sophie Vanderhooven step out of a Lincoln, Dexter behind her. She supposed she should have known Sophie would bring a stand-in for her fiancé who was still working in Italy.

Since she felt it would be rude to drive by a paying client, she drew to a stop and rolled down her window. The autumn day was crisp and cold and tonight the temperature was forecast to dip.

"You look lovely, Sophie," she said. The blue woolen suit was both stylish and classic, rather like Sophie herself.

"Thanks. I can't wait to see Melissa get married."

"Do you drive away before all the ceremonies?" Dex asked her.

Now that he'd addressed her directly, she had to look at him and nothing in the world could stop the warm blush that heated her cheeks as their little tussle in her office roared back to her.

She forced a smile, though no one could have called it cool. "Of course not. Just a little wedding business to take care of. I'll see you later." And with a wave of her hand she drove past.

DEX SQUINTED as he turned to watch Karen drive away. He'd made her blush. Good. It was a start.

"What's going on, Dex?"

He turned back to his date. "What do you mean?"

Sophie scanned his face. "I'm not sure, but you were looking at Karen the way—well, the way Andrew looks at me. I guess that's why I recognized the expression."

"She's a very attractive woman."

"And she was blushing." She grabbed his hand and began walking toward the church. "And there's this sort of energy field when you two are together. I noticed it when we first met her. I wasn't born yesterday, Dex. Something's up with you two. What is it?"

The slim hand in his was friendly, but firm. He suspected he wouldn't get away with anything but the truth. "You're pretty smart for a socialite."

"I know. And I smell a delicious secret. Come on, spill. I won't tell anyone."

"I've never yet met a woman who didn't break that promise."

The patrician nose wrinkled. "Can I tell Andrew if it's good?"

Andrew was the son of a famous wine-making family in Italy. He'd hired Dexter's firm to renovate the family's Park Avenue town house and during the project, the two had become friends. They played squash, moved in similar social circles and, instead of dropping him when Andrew and Sophie got engaged, the couple had tried setting him up with a series of single women.

They knew he'd been married before, but he'd never offered them much in the way of details. Hadn't thought it would matter. Now, he knew that his past did matter.

The past had just caught up with him.

"The truth is that Karen and I used to be married."

If he was into shocking people he'd have been gratified by the way Sophie's mouth fell open so far he could see all her expensive dental work. He'd never seen a mouth with such perfectly straight molars.

When she'd recovered enough to close her mouth,

she said, "But I don't get it. Why? What?" She heaved a sigh. "What's your plan?"

The pavement seemed to tick under Sophie's heels, sounding like a clock counting seconds. "I don't know. Honestly, I didn't have a plan. Don't have one. I thought it would be cool to surprise Karen, but—"

"The force field got to you." She shook her head. "That is some powerful chemistry between you two."

She was right. The moment Karen had stepped out of her office and he'd seen her again, he'd known that what they'd had wasn't over. Not for him. "Yeah."

"So, what happened between you two?"

"We should go in."

"That's Melissa's dad over there looking all stressed. Means the bridal party isn't here yet. We've got some time." She hauled him around the side of the church. "Spill."

The story was so stupid he felt foolish even repeating it. "This drunk woman came onto me at a party and Karen flipped out. She got it in her head that I was cheating on her."

Cool blue eyes stared into his. "Were you?"

"No. I never would have done anything like that to Karen. I loved my wife."

"Then why would she think it?"

He leaned his back against the brick wall. It seemed sturdy, solid, the way a good marriage should be. "I've spent a lot of time asking myself the same question."

"How badly was the drunk woman coming onto you?"

"Oh, it was bad. She was undressing herself, trying to undress me. When Karen walked in on us she was plastered to me, and I was trying to stop her unzipping me. Must have looked to Karen like we were in a big hurry, both trying to get me unzipped." He'd never really looked at it from her point of view before. He'd been too busy being pissed that she didn't believe him.

"Wow. That sucks."

"I know."

"Did you go for counseling?"

"The only counselor she wanted was the kind in a lawyer's office. She started divorce proceedings right after she threw me out of the house."

"Why would she end a marriage without even fighting for it?"

Leaning against the brick of that old church he felt like a little of the wisdom of the aged building was seeping into him. "Her dad really ran around on her mom. For years, with a lot of different women, until her mom finally divorced the jerk. Maybe, on some level, Karen expects a husband to be unfaithful."

"Then you're going to have to figure out how to convince her that some husbands can love a woman faithfully. And that you are one of them."

"We're already divorced. Why would I do that?"

When she shook her head at him, the sun struck her pale blond hair, giving him the impression of a halo. "No wonder you never looked twice at any of those women I introduced you to." She patted his shoulder. "You, my friend, are still in love with your wife."

KAREN FOUND the best man without trouble. He was the only guy in a tux standing on the freeway looking miserable.

She pulled over. "Hop in," she said. Then, before pulling back into traffic, she made contact with her limo driver. "Where are you?"

"Five minutes away."

"Make it ten."

"You got it."

She delivered a very grateful best man to an equally grateful groom and breathed a sigh of relief. Then she dashed to the front of the church to welcome the bridal party. As she'd suspected, they had no idea they'd been stalled.

The bride was as radiant as could be hoped, and after escorting her and the bridesmaids to where her father waited, adjusting her veil and reminding everyone to take a deep breath and smile, to remember to savor the walk down the aisle, she slipped inside to give the organist the heads up.

As the strains of "Here Comes the Bride" boomed through the church, everyone rose. In her head she heard her own personal musical mash-up, the wedding march overlaid with her own version of "Another One Bites the Dust."

Once the wedding was underway, she eased back out of the church and called Chelsea who was already preparing food for the reception. "Heads up. We're running behind about fifteen minutes."

"'Kay, thanks." And the woman was gone.

She then drove to the mansion where the reception was being held. The kitchen was a hive of organized chaos. Chelsea overseeing the sit-down dinner for one hundred and fifty that would take place as soon as the guests arrived.

She walked into the huge ballroom-turned-dining room and was filled with pleasure. It looked beautiful. They'd gone with autumnal colors and the burgundies and golds and greens looked lovely against the rich mahogany wainscoting in the room. Real fires already burned in the two fireplaces and bouquets of autumn leaves, artfully arranged to look casual and natural adorned the space. Fat candles waited to be lit, the crystal shone, the cutlery glittered, and Cinderella's confectionary coach lent a whimsical touch.

Dee called her when the bride and groom were on their way, so she was at the front door to greet them.

"We did it," Melissa cried, holding up her left hand where a brand-new band glittered.

"Congratulations," she said, hugging the happy young woman. "I've got rooms upstairs for both of you so you can freshen up. Once all the guests have arrived, we'll announce you and the reception can begin."

She took the extra ring that the groom pressed secretively into her palm, slipping it onto her right hand once more for safekeeping.

As with most weddings, the guests enjoying the perfect event could have no idea of the infinite number of details handled and the disasters averted that went on behind the scenes. And that was exactly how Karen liked it.

So she was less than pleased when Dexter surprised her at the end of the evening when most of the guests had departed.

"You do good work," he said. "I'm truly impressed."

"I thought you'd gone," she snapped, then could have cursed her tongue for betraying that she'd noticed when Sophie left and assumed Dex was with her.

"I told Sophie I had a ride." He shrugged, looking impossibly gorgeous in a well-cut suit in shale gray.

"Do you?"

"I do if you give me a lift, otherwise I guess I'll call a cab."

"Why didn't you go home with your date?"

"Because she's not a date. She's the fiancée of a good friend. I didn't want anybody thinking there was something going on between me and Sophie when there isn't." He held her gaze. "You know how suspicious people can be."

Refusing to rise to such obvious bait she said, "Well, I guess I can give you a lift but you'll have to wait until I'm finished here."

"No problem. Can I make myself useful?"

"You can help load the supplies into the van." In fact, she hired a company to take care of the cleanup, but she was annoyed with Dexter and half hoped he got something nasty on his pretty suit.

As though he'd read her mind, he slipped off his jacket, and, to her surprise, slipped it over her shoulders. "Take care of that for me." Then he rolled up his sleeves and headed toward the cleanup crew, turning quickly from wedding guest to menial laborer.

The jacket was warm from his body and, weak woman that she was, she slipped her arms into the sleeves and enjoyed the sensation of wearing something of his. She caught an elusive scent of him, something hot and spicy and forbidden.

Then she went into the kitchen to check in with Chelsea. Her caterer was pretty much ready to go, the kitchen cleaner than when she'd arrived and all her food and supplies loaded into her van.

"How you doing?"

"My feet hurt." She grinned. "But we pulled off another miracle."

"I thought the Cinderella coach cake was a bit much, but everyone seemed to like it."

"Seems we're never too old for fairy tales."

"Speaking of fairy tales, who's the Prince Charming out there hauling tables and why are you wearing his jacket?"

"That's no prince, that's my ex-husband." She didn't bother to explain the other part.

"Wow." Chelsea did a double take, and she followed her friend's gaze to the sight of her ex's delectable backside as he bent over, helping lift a heavy table. "That's the scumbag? Too bad he's a wretched human being. He sure looks good."

"Yeah."

They both watched out the window for a few more moments. "He doesn't mind getting his hands dirty, I'll give him that."

"No." She'd always loved that about him, the architect who was only too happy to get down and dirty with the construction aspects of his projects. She was never sure whether he appealed to her more when he was designing and envisioning a finished project, or when he was covered in sweat and sawdust, muscles bulging.

Chelsea pulled herself away from the window first. "Okay, I've got my own eye candy at home. I'd better get back, David's waiting for me."

"Sure. Have a great Sunday." They hugged quickly.

She was, as usual, the last one to leave. Only this time, she wasn't alone. Dexter followed her to her car. The temperature had dropped suddenly and there was a sharp chill in the air.

Once they were settled into her car, the heater humming, she turned to him and said, "So, where can I drop you?"

He gazed at her mouth. "I was hoping we could pick up where we left off the other night."

5

"WHAT?" The word bounced around the inside of her car, even though her shock was only pretense. She'd known the moment Dexter asked her for a ride home that he had more than transportation in mind. You didn't love a man for six years, live with him for five, without knowing a thing or two about how his mind worked.

Or have him know about how yours worked, she realized, as he gazed at her separated by nothing but a couple of feet of cold air, with an expression that suggested he knew she was as aware of him as he was of her. "Come on," he said. "You've been thinking about having sex with me, too. I know you're too honest to pretend you haven't."

Which was exactly what she'd planned to do. Deny, deny, deny. She sighed out a breath of mingled frustration and—no, it was all frustration, both the irritation of a woman dealing with a man she thought was out of her life, and the huge dollop of sexual frustration that being around Dex again was causing. Because she couldn't be near him and not remember how they'd burned up the sheets together. No matter their problems, their sex life had always been superb.

"I can't—"

"Whatever else was wrong between us, you can't deny that when we got naked, everything worked," he said, oddly echoing her own thoughts on the matter. Then he reached over, and ran a fingertip under the hem of her skirt. "Or not even naked," he mused, his eyes crinkling as memories rose around them. "Remember that time when we took my first brand-new car out for a spin?"

"No," she lied.

Which was a huge mistake because then, of course, he had to remind her of an incident they both knew she remembered perfectly well.

"I'd only ever driven used beaters, and now suddenly I had a company car, and it was brand-new. We went to the dealership to pick it up. A silver GM sedan." It had been a green Ford, but she refused to rise to the bait no matter how provocatively he behaved. She shifted an inch closer to her door, but he shifted, too, so his finger continued to trace the hem of her skirt which had, naturally, ridden up when she sat down. She could smack him away, but that would make an issue of something she preferred to ignore. Besides, what he was doing felt so good, and it had been so long.

"It was summer and you wore a red sundress." He was right about the season, but she'd worn a blue cotton dress. She never wore red with her hair color. His wandering finger had reached the crease of her closed legs and he paused for a second. "Is any of this familiar?"

"Not ringing any bells yet." Ha.

His voice grew husky. "We took a drive, didn't know

where we were going, didn't care. We found ourselves down by the river. It was quiet, nobody around."

Because he'd obviously carefully done a reconnaissance mission beforehand. When he'd pulled out a bottle of wine from his briefcase along with two glasses, she'd known it.

"Do you remember what happened then?" he asked, his voice so close, so deep and low, that she knew he'd moved closer.

"No," she lied.

"That's too bad. I'll never forget that night as long as I live."

The touch of his finger doing no more than trace her hem, running along her upper thigh, was so erotic it was an act of will not to squirm, not to push his hand higher, where she needed release so desperately, or at least depress the handy button that would recline their seats. Or even better, act as they had that night he was describing, and simply crawl into the backseat where there was more room.

"I'm sure you've made lots of new memories since then," she snapped.

"Don't you want to know what happened?" he asked her, as though she'd never spoken.

"It was a long time ago."

"Not that long."

Maybe she could force her body to remain still while that one finger played at her hem, never going higher or doing anything that would make it necessary for her to slap him down, but she couldn't seem to control her breathing. Even as she tried to pretend she felt nothing, remembered nothing, a combination of his finger stroking her skin, his nearness, and the sweet, painful pull of memory was causing her breathing to speed up along with her pulse.

"We talked about my new job, and a new event you were organizing, and it seemed like we could do anything. We were young, smart, ambitious and we had each other. What an unbeatable team." The finger stalled for a moment and she felt the tension in his hand as though a spasm of emotion had hit him. It felt like anger, but she had to assume it was guilt for throwing everything they'd had away.

Then the moment passed and the back-and-forth exploration of her thigh continued. He tugged her skirt up a full half inch, torturing her again with a slow track back, his finger pad tracing a line of heat across her skin.

"All the while we talked, I did this. Played at your hem, and you pretended you didn't notice, like now."

"I think your memory's playing tricks."

"And then, suddenly, you parted your legs and turned toward me." He swallowed. So did she. Heat flooded her body as she remembered what came next.

"I thought I was so in control, touching you, turning us both on, but you were the one in control, weren't you? You were the one with the secret."

"No," she whispered, but she wasn't telling him she hadn't had a secret, she was trying to stop the flood of memory that was as warm and thick as desire.

"When I got up to touch your panties, you weren't wearing any."

Oh, how she remembered. The feel of the air wafting up her skirt, the wanton knowledge that she'd stood by while he'd finalized paperwork at a car dealership, while they'd driven public highways, and all the time, underneath her cotton sundress, she'd been bare-assed.

"We were in the backseat so fast I ended up with bruised elbows and knees. We never did take off our clothes, did we? I ended up flipping that skirt up, pulling down the top of your dress to reach your breasts. You were always so sensitive there." He laughed softly. "We were like a pair of kids going at it." He sighed, obviously realizing that this little trip down memory lane wasn't working. Her thighs didn't ease open, though he couldn't possibly know what torture it was to hold them closed against him. "God, I loved you."

"But not enough," she said, her voice so soft she wasn't sure if he'd heard her.

"Do you think we rushed into marriage too fast?"

She turned her head, wondering where he was going with this train of thought. "We knew each other a year. I guess I wish we'd waited. Long enough for me to realize you weren't the kind of guy to stick with one woman."

He pulled his hand back into his own lap and she fought the urge to grab it and put it where she needed, so urgently, to be touched.

"I wish I'd waited long enough to get a handle on those demons you carry around with you."

"What demons?" she snapped. How like a man to cheat on her and then try and pretend she was the one with the problem.

"The demons that stopped you being able to trust."

She was not going to have this conversation again. She'd moved on. "If I'm so full of demons, what are you doing still trying to get into my pants?"

A sigh of pure frustration rolled through him. "Hell if I know."

6

THE READING TERMINAL MARKET was crazy. Naturally. It was a Sunday afternoon and every yuppie with a craving for organic arugula or some fresh monkfish had made tracks down here. Karen had a love/hate relationship with the market. While she loved this place simply for the fun of people-watching, she also suffered as only a woman who loves food and tries to live on fifteen hundred calories a day can suffer.

Since she'd barely slept thanks to Dex and his antics in her car last night, she felt weaker than usual. The worst part had been driving him to his hotel, with all the steamy atmosphere between them churning around with a lot of emotions. Anger, frustration, and a bitter kind of longing that hurt more than all the other feelings put together. How could she still want the man so much?

Dex was her ex. He had to remain that way if she had any chance of hanging on to her hard-won self-esteem.

She'd half thought he'd invite her up to his room and was ready to let him have it when he did. Somehow, the fact that he didn't say any more than, "Thanks for the ride. Night," was an added insult. He didn't even ask her up to his room so she could annihilate the guy with a few well-chosen words that she'd been practicing for blocks.

How unfair was that?

The bakery smells were so good. There were blocks of cheese bigger than house steps and she wanted to buy one and gobble every succulent morsel. She loved cheese, every fat-saturated ounce. Hard cheese, soft cheese, runny cheese, blue cheese. Oh, stop it. She averted her eyes. She really shouldn't be here.

But Ron had suggested the locale for their first coffee date and, under instruction from Dee, she'd agreed without quibbling. Now she was here she wished she'd quibbled big-time. She wanted to turn tail and head home. Apart from being exhausted, cranky and cheese-obsessed, she'd probably dressed all wrong for a first date with a stranger. Her jeans were casual, but she'd pushed her feet into high heels instead of giving them a well-deserved Sunday rest, and she was worried that the green sweater was too low-necked. The last thing she wanted to do was stick her boobs in some poor man's face, so she'd added a scarf at the last moment, and now wished she could go home and start over.

Dee had made her promise to let her hair down, which she'd first assumed was some kind of veiled allusion to being open for sex with a stranger until Dee had clarified that she actually meant she should leave her hair unpinned and unconfined. "You have such great hair, that gorgeous red color and the natural curls." And since Dee seemed to know what she was doing in the online dating world, Karen had been persuaded.

Now she suddenly felt like a country-and-western

singer with too much of everything. Big hair, big heels, big breasts, big butt.

She was a few minutes early, because it was her way, and stopped to stare unseeing at a booth selling nothing but spices. She never should have agreed to this date with Ron the CPA.

Somehow, this was all Dexter's fault. If he hadn't got her so riled up she never would have agreed to a date with some guy she met over the Internet.

However, she realized that whatever her reasons for being here, she wasn't about to stand this man up. It wasn't his fault she was an idiot. So, they'd have coffee. An hour of her life would be wasted, and then she could get back to attempting to make something of the years left to her.

On that optimistic thought, she made her way to the busy coffee shop and immediately spotted Ron, who was standing near the entrance, obviously as punctual as she was.

He looked exactly like his photo. Exactly like a CPA. And suddenly she relaxed. He was reassuringly unassuming, no other women were covertly studying him or overtly drooling. He was the kind of man who wouldn't forever be tempted to stray, which had to be a good thing.

She forced a smile to her face and walked up to him. "Hello, you must be Ron. I'm Karen."

They shook hands. He seemed pleased by her punctuality, insisted on buying her a coffee and they settled at a table.

For a moment, neither spoke. Finally he said, "You're very punctual. It's a quality I admire."

Oh, how old-fashioned he sounded. What was she even doing here? Her mind flashed back to the night before, when she'd been humiliatingly close to parting her thighs and doing her ex-husband in the parking lot. Something had to change, and fast. She smiled at him. "I feel the same way."

Now that she looked at him, she saw that behind his glasses he had warm gray eyes. He was fairly forgettable until you took note of those eyes. He was dressed neatly, in jeans that bore such sharp creases she suspected he ironed them, a polo shirt he'd probably bought at Costco or Sam's Club and a well-worn leather jacket.

Another pause ensued, while they both took refuge in sipping coffee, and finally she blurted, "I have no idea how to do this. I'm so sorry, it's my first time." She sighed, sensing the genuine niceness of this man, and opened up even more. "In fact, it's been a long time since I had any kind of a date. I'm so out of practice I have no idea where to begin."

It was as though her confession took all the awkwardness out of their date. Ron nodded with sweet understanding. "It sucks. Really."

She was surprised into a spurt of laughter by his sad admission.

Then realizing how that must sound, he added, "I don't mean meeting you, but online dating is a new skill you have to learn." He shrugged. "I've been doing this for a few months now and I find the hardest part is that people often, when they write their profiles, put a description of what they wish they were like rather than something that's actually true."

She thought of the way she'd fudged her height, claiming to be five-four, and tried very hard not to blush.

"The worst thing for me was the bad spelling and grammar. I don't think I'm too fussy, but if a man can't spell *relationship,* I really don't think I want to have one with him."

"True. For me the biggest turnoff is women who are so obviously looking for the father of their future children that they all but ask you for a sperm count."

Once again she laughed, sensing that maybe he wasn't quite as dull as he appeared. "I've tried very hard to be honest," he said.

"You told me all about your work," she reminded him, "but very little about yourself."

"There's not much to tell. I'm thirty-seven. Single, I'm a CPA."

"Whoa," she said. "We're getting back to your résumé again."

"Sorry. I'm not one to wear my heart on my sleeve."

"Whereabouts do you live?" she asked, seeking for some topic that they could talk about.

"I'm within walking distance of Independence Hall," he said and she wondered if he was being deliberately vague in case she turned out to be a stalker or crazy person.

"Wow. In Society Hill? That's a nice area."

He paused for a second, then said, "I inherited the house from my mother. It's a Federal-style town house. She recently passed."

"I'm so sorry," she said with ready sympathy. She couldn't imagine life without her mother, who was both nosy and annoying and the person who loved Karen most in all the world.

"Cancer," he said. "It was very hard."

She heard the almost hidden quiver in his voice and impulsively reached over to lay a hand on his. Because she didn't know what to say, she said nothing, merely offered her silent support.

After a second, he said, "My only regret is that she didn't get to see me settled, with grandchildren. It was her dearest wish."

"I'm sure she was very proud of you." She searched for something else to say. "Do you have brothers and sisters?"

"No, I'm an only child." And she received the impression that he'd been his mother's pride and joy. She didn't ask, but she suspected he'd never left home, had nursed his mother through her final illness and now, lost and alone, was trying to find a substitute.

"How about you?" he asked, obviously determined to steer clear of painful subjects.

"I'm divorced." She didn't think he wanted to hear the ugly details. Well, who would? So she merely said, "I've been single for almost five years now. I run my own wedding planning business."

He began asking her precise and intelligent questions about her business and she felt that it was a relief to both of them to discuss something as impersonal as business.

At the end of an hour, she knew two things. One, Ron was a genuinely nice man, she suspected he was an excellent accountant, and two, she felt not the tiniest spark of attraction.

They exchanged business cards and agreed to meet for lunch one day soon. She had no idea whether either of them would follow up, but she was toying with the idea of hiring him for her business.

They shook hands at the end of their coffee date and he headed one way while she turned in the opposite direction.

She was trying to decide whether the coffee date had been a success or a disaster, when a voice hailed her, "Karen."

She glanced up to see Chelsea standing in front of her, a canvas bag of fresh food in her arms. Beside her was her fiancé, David, loaded down with two more bags. She was struck with how good those two looked together, two tall, gorgeous people who were so clearly meant for each other you could feel their bond.

After the greetings were over, Chelsea turned to her lover and said, "David, do you see that fish market way over there?"

He glanced at his woman with slightly raised brows. "You mean the one with the long lineup?"

"That's the one. Can you go buy six spot prawns and a pound of fresh crabmeat?"

He glanced from one woman to the other. "You wouldn't be trying to get rid of me, so you can do the girlfriend gossip thing, would you?"

Chelsea grinned at him. "Do you want what I can whip up with six spot prawns and a pound of crabmeat or don't you?"

With a good-natured shrug, he said, "Goodbye, Karen." And wandered off.

"That was rude. We'll see each other at work tomorrow."

"I can't wait until tomorrow. Believe me, he'll end up happy when his dinner is served. And I have to hear about your date."

She made a wry face. "He was really nice. A truly nice man."

"That sounds very unpromising."

"It's not his fault. I wouldn't even be doing this if it

wasn't for Dee, my darling assistant who seems to think I'm in desperate need of a man."

"She's young, what does she know?"

Karen snorted. "She thinks she knows more than I do. Know what I found on my desk Friday morning?"

"What?"

"A box of condoms and a note from Dee reminding me to always play it safe."

Chelsea had the kind of full-bodied laugh that made strangers stop and grin as though just being around her made them part of the fun. "What did you do with them?"

"I put them in my desk drawer. I have everything in there from hemorrhoid cream, which is good for minimizing puffy eyes on brides and their mothers before a photo shoot, to extra nylons, shoelaces, pins, tape, flower wire, film, batteries, hair spray, you name it."

"And now you've got condoms." She leaned closer so none of the fresh fruit and veggie shoppers would overhear her. "Maybe the CPA will get to sharpen his pencil after all."

She snorted with her own, hardly dainty laughter. "Stop it. I'm thinking of hiring him to do my books. We talked a lot about my business, it was an easy subject for both of us and he asked intelligent questions."

"Oh, poor guy. So the date was a disaster."

She wondered what Chelsea was planning to do with that dark green spiky stuff sticking out of her bag and decided she didn't want to know. "No, I wouldn't say he was a disaster, just there was no big spark, you know?"

"Oh, yeah. I know. But maybe he's worth giving

another chance, seeing as sometimes people we spark off aren't always good for us."

"I so agree."

Her friend drilled her with her gaze. "Speaking of bad news and sparks, how's Dex the Ex?"

$$7$$

DEXTER WAS A SUCKER for punishment. He knew it, could curse himself as much as he liked, but all the cursing didn't stop him from pulling up in front of Karen's office for the latest wedding planning meeting. He'd had to cut short an earlier meeting with the developers of the mixed use complex he was designing in order to be here. He'd been far more delighted to bag this project than he should have been and he suspected his level of satisfaction was related to the fact that he'd be spending a lot of time in Philadelphia for the next few months.

In missile range of the redheaded termagant he'd so foolishly married.

It wasn't like his buddy Andrew and Sophie couldn't have a perfectly good wedding without him playing assistant wedding planner.

And yet, here he was.

He pulled in to park in the office lot and there was Karen's car. A surprising shot of lust pummeled him as he recalled their all-too-short time together Saturday night when her mouth had told him *no* even as her body shouted *yes*.

What was he going to do about this very inconvenient thing he still had for his ex-wife?

Until he figured that out, he supposed he was going to play assistant wedding planner.

He was a few minutes early and it didn't look as if Sophie was here yet, but they'd booked the last possible appointment so they could both get in a day's work. Probably she'd be here any minute.

Loosening his tie, he went into the office anyway. He glanced around but the cute British girl wasn't at her station or anywhere in the front area of If You Can Dream It. He walked toward Karen's office and heard her voice. He was conscious of the familiarity of that voice, the slight breathlessness that he doubted she was even aware of. His day had been successful, the client had approved the more expensive option, the one Dexter had hoped they'd go with since it was both greener and preserved the architectural integrity of the building.

There was a time he'd have rushed to tell her the good news and they'd have celebrated. Now they were all but strangers to each other. And yet he knew every timbre of her voice as well as he knew every inch of her body. It was crazy.

When he got to her doorway he paused there, enjoying the view. She was talking on the phone, her bare feet up on the desktop, a sight he suspected not very many clients were privileged to see. Her feet were small, dainty, the toes painted bright pink. Her floral skirt had ridden up revealing a shapely thigh.

He rapped on the door frame and she turned, startled. When she saw him, she yanked her feet off the desktop and he watched, enjoying the sight, as her toes did a version of Riverdance under the desk until she located two high-heeled shoes and attempted to jam her feet into them while simultaneously dragging her skirt back into place.

She continued her conversation, to a florist he presumed, since the words *rose* and *baby's breath* occurred so often.

Once she'd successfully navigated her feet into her shoes, she turned her chair, and thus her back, to him and continued her conversation. "What about the ribbon? Were you able to match the color of the bridesmaids' dresses?" He watched her pick up the pen he'd given her and begin to doodle. "Mmm-hmm. Okay. I know it's a difficult color to match, but the bride is very particular about tone." She made a quick note. "Well, I think you should send over a sample of the ribbon and we can let the bride decide. Yes, I know. Right. See you." And she hung up.

She let him stand there another moment while she made notes. Then she turned her chair so she was facing him.

"Hi," he said.

"Didn't Sophie get hold of you?" his ex-wife asked, rising and coming to stand in front of her desk.

He'd had his cell phone turned off while he was on-site with the client. Had he remembered to turn it back on? He didn't think so. "Why?"

"She got held up at work. She rescheduled our meeting."

"Oh." He pulled out his cell phone and when he turned it on, there was the little voice mail icon. "Guess I forgot to check my messages."

"Guess so."

She didn't move. If there was a posture for "there's

the door, don't let it hit you on your way out," she was demonstrating it. But he'd known this woman for a long time, and during the best of that time, intimately, and he knew she was skittish because she didn't want to be alone with him. Not when they both knew that the fire that had always burned between them hadn't grown fainter from time apart. If anything, it burned fiercer than ever.

Ever since that kiss the other night he'd been thinking that it was inevitable they'd end up back in bed.

He glanced at that sturdy-looking desk. Or not in bed.

"Has your assistant left for the day?"

"Yep, and I'm finished for the day, too, so I'll let you know when the meeting's rescheduled." She stuck out her hand for him to shake.

Maybe if she hadn't done that he would have walked away as she was pretending she wanted him to. But offering her hand like he was a casual business acquaintance?

She might as well have flipped him the bird.

He took her hand. Held it in his for a moment too long, felt the quiver running along her skin, the soft warmth of their palm-to-palm contact. Not letting go of her hand he took a step toward her.

She stepped back.

He took another step toward her.

"Dex, what are you…" Her hips bumped the desk and their gazes locked.

He watched the quick intake of breath, the way it raised her glorious, extravagant breasts against the silk of her blouse. Her mouth opened slightly and he moved in, taking her mouth as though he owned it because on some primitive level he did. Always had. Always would.

The sweet taste of her exploded on his lips and tongue and then he pulled her in all the way, tight against him so her breasts were pressing against his chest, her hips jammed against him, her butt pressed against the edge of her feminine desk.

For a second he felt her go rigid, thought she might push him away, but as quickly as her resistance rose, it receded and with a low moan in the back of her throat, she pushed her hands into his hair, pulled him into her.

He'd always loved her honest passion, the way she let him know what she was feeling and what she wanted. Mindless, they pulled at each other, the years of separation, the anger, the frustration falling away as they clawed at each other.

He had his hands shoved down her top, grabbing at her breasts, pulling them out of her bra so he could see them, feel them, taste them. She'd always been slightly embarrassed about the size of her breasts but he loved them. When he put his tongue to her nipple the flavor took him back to the first time they'd ever been together, when he'd discovered this woman was made for sex. Or, as he secretly liked to think, she was made for sex with him.

Her head dropped back as he curled his tongue around the sensitive point, pushed his knee between her legs until she parted for him. Without taking his mouth from her breast he reached under her hips and hoisted her up until she sat on the desk, her pretty floral skirt sliding up as he pushed it up, up, over her hips. She spread herself wide for him, her arms twined around his neck, her head thrown back as he pleasured her.

The joy of this woman was how well he knew her body, how intimately he could gauge her responses. Beneath his tongue her skin was heating and he could feel her pulse hammering. When he trailed a hand down between her thighs he found her as wet and hot as he'd suspected he would. He cupped her, making her moan and squirm against his fingers.

"It's been so long," he murmured against her plump flesh.

"Too long," she moaned.

Slipping his hands beneath her hips, he peeled the tiny scrap of pale blue silk and lace that passed for underwear off her, bending as he slid the foolish thing down her legs and over the ridiculous heels. He was throbbing with need, so aroused he was in danger of embarrassing himself as he rose and slid open his zipper.

She reached between them, unbuttoning him and sliding her small, capable hands around him which didn't help his self-control.

While she caressed him he returned the favor, cupping her heat, slipping one finger into that glorious wet until she squirmed against him. He knew her so well, he knew that she was as close to exploding as he was.

He looked down into her face, her eyes that clear blue-green, her cheeks flushed with passion, a sprinkle of freckles across her nose and cheeks, her lips parted and eager. He closed the distance between them, kissing her hungrily.

Had he ever wanted her this much? Had he ever wanted anyone or anything this badly? If so, he couldn't remember.

She pulled him closer and as he touched the wet heat he suddenly checked himself as reality intruded. They weren't married anymore. He had no idea if she was on birth control or what she'd been doing since they were last together. With a groan of gut-deep frustration he cursed himself for no longer carrying a condom in his wallet. But he wasn't a kid anymore. The only prophylactics he owned were safely in his bedside drawer at home.

Pulling away slightly, then resting his forehead against hers, he admitted the awful truth. "I don't have protection," he gasped.

"Oh, no...wait, I've got some condoms in my desk drawer."

"Really?"

"Yeah. On top of the hair spray, I think."

He bounded around the desk and flung open the drawer. The oddest assortment of products greeted him. He dug around and found the unopened box wedged between a can of breath spray and a tube of Preparation H.

Whatever.

He didn't let himself think about why his ex-wife kept a box of condoms in her desk drawer, simply decided to be grateful.

He tore into the box and swiftly sheathed himself, then holding his pants up with one hand, made his way back around to where his ex-wife still sat, leaning back, supported by her hands, still open for him.

Waiting.

He didn't keep her waiting for long. Teasing her with his fingers, toying with her until her breathing grew shallow and raspy and she was moving against him, he brought her up and then pulling her hips to the edge of the desk, he stepped between her thighs and slowly eased into her. Oh, it felt so good, so right. He'd forgotten how amazing she was. Snug heat, the sweet slide as she thrust against him, the crazy dance she did with her hips when her excitement began to peak, pumping and corkscrewing around him until he had no resistance left.

Their mouths fused, their hearts pounded in sync and he thrust up and home again and again while she danced and pumped against him.

She lost control, began to pant, to moan and gyrate her hips crazily.

"Yes," he whispered, loving the way she let herself go completely.

"Oh, Dex," she cried, and then he felt the spasms clutch at him even as her head fell back and she cried out in ecstasy.

He stroked in and out of her slowly, easing her through her orgasm and then she opened her eyes, unfocused and huge and with a tiny moan, she grabbed his hips and thrust against him again, driving herself to a second climax and taking him along for the ride.

No way to hold back when she grabbed his ass like that, squeezing and pulling him into paradise even as she continued that crazy corkscrew thing with her hips. He was lost, and when she came the second time, he cried out in unison.

For a few minutes they remained slumped against each other, panting. Sweat dotted her upper chest and her mouth was swollen from their passion.

He didn't want to pull out of her body, loved the feel of all that snug heat wrapped around him, still pulsing with aftershocks, their bodies close and intimate.

At last she leaned back and glanced up at him, a half-embarrassed grin splitting her face. "That wasn't quite the meeting I planned."

"It's always been best between us when it was spontaneous," he reminded her. When he thought of some of the places they'd done it, half-derelict buildings he was working on, a Finnish sauna that time he'd almost passed out, his parents' garden shed. Her office after hours seemed pretty tame.

She gazed at him through slumberous eyes that sent him so many messages he wanted to take her all over again. His breathing wasn't quite steady, his pulse nowhere near slowing.

"Next time," she said.

Oh, yes, if she was talking next time then he hadn't completely blown any chance he might have with her by acting like a Neanderthal.

He liked the sexy half smile on her face.

"Next time? What? Do you have any special requests? Positions, locales, maybe a toy you'd like to try?"

As though she'd made up her mind about something, she leaned back and said, "Who needs toys when I've got you?"

A toy? Shock held him speechless. She was planning to treat him like a battery-operated pleasure tool? The kind he saw in sex shops in a million girlie colors. Oh, wasn't that just great. He'd planned to invite her out for dinner, maybe try to talk to her and instead she was treating him like he had multi-speeds and a rotating head.

She pulled up her legs and swung around and off her desk, as graceful as a dancer. "What I was going to say was, 'next time, maybe you could take your tie off.'"

8

I had a very nice time, the e-mail said. Perhaps we could do it again sometime.

Karen stared at the words and felt ridiculously guilty. She didn't owe Ron anything. All they'd shared was coffee, but the fact that she'd shared completely inappropriate desktop sex with Dexter only a day after her date with the CPA filled her with remorse and that translated into an odd feeling of guilt where Ron was concerned.

Not knowing how to answer or what to say, she closed her computer and did what she too often did in times of stress. She walked over to Chelsea's place.

But it turned out she wasn't the only one acting uncharacteristically crazy. When she got there, before she could open her mouth and wail out her troubles, her caterer and friend put a finger over her lips and beckoned her to follow.

Wondering if her complete lunacy was perhaps catching, she warily followed Chelsea who crept toward the industrial kitchen she shared with Laurel, the cake designer. Stealthily opening the door, she quietly beckoned Karen into the kitchen ahead of her.

And then Karen realized why she'd acted so secretive.

Laurel was in the throes of creation.

Laurel wasn't a woman who worked in a normal way. In fact there was little about Laurel that was exactly mainstream. She was a wraithlike creature who tended to wear gauzy clothes and Indian cottons. She practiced yoga and had spent more time than was probably good for her in an ashram.

She was as insubstantial as gossamer, as unworldly as a nun, as hard to pin down as a cloud.

But her cakes were pure magic.

An artist whose media were devil's food and fondant and royal icing and marzipan and heaven knew what else, she was a joy to watch, though easily distracted, so both women stood quietly watching as she painted food coloring onto whimsical flowers. The cake itself was a child's fantasy of fairies and strangely shaped trees, animals and a pair of dainty children.

They left the kitchen as quietly as they'd entered it. "What's the occasion?" Karen asked.

"It's a fundraiser for a children's shelter. She volunteered the cake."

Karen shook her head fondly. "It's a good thing she has us or she'd never make any money."

"I know. She truly is the most airy-fairy person I've ever met. Can you imagine how she could clean up in New York or L.A. if she had any ambition?"

"I do have ambition," a soft voice said behind them. Laurel moved as quietly as the fairies she loved to create and seemed neither surprised nor offended to find them talking about her. "I want every cake to tell a story." She removed the scarf she'd wrapped around her multicolored hair and shrugged out of the plain white apron that always seemed much too big and heavy for her slight frame. "I'm just not into material success."

"I know, honey," Karen said. "We weren't criticizing you. We love you."

"I know." She turned suddenly, her waifish look vanishing in a mischievous grin. "And it's a lot easier to pay my rent since you two took over my billings." She rolled her neck and then did a few shoulder exercises. "Would you like to see my sketches for the circus wedding cake?"

"Love to."

Laurel dug a well-worn sketchbook from her hand-woven bag. She flipped through the book and showed them a watercolor drawing of the cake.

"This is why you are a genius," Chelsea exclaimed when they looked at the drawing. "I'd have gone with a circus tent probably, or tightrope walkers or something to suggest a circus."

Karen nodded.

"Too mundane," the young woman replied.

What she'd created was difficult to describe. She'd drawn a tower of diminishing-sized cake layers that grew narrower as the cake grew taller, so it felt as though the cake might disappear into the clouds. From the top she'd drawn an explosion of multicolored ribbons cascading like fireworks.

"Will these be ribbons?" Karen asked, wondering how she'd get ribbon to contort into those shapes and stay there.

"No. Gum paste. That's sugar with natural gum that feels like Play-Doh but dries hard. It holds its shape so I can get icing ribbons to curl and dance."

"Amazing. And I know that's fondant, right?" Karen added, having worked with Laurel long enough to know how much she liked to cover her cake with the smooth icing which she could paint, often using a special airbrush tool. The cake design was like an abstract painting, with reds and purples, blues and greens, and bright splotches of yellow all clashing and intermingling. Somehow she suggested movement through color. Without including a single circus element, she'd caught the energy of Cirque du Soleil. "It's brilliant," Karen agreed.

"Glad you like it. I'll probably add a few elements, but this is the basic idea." She stuffed the book into her bag. "Well, I've got to go to my Vinyasa flow class. See you later." And she was gone.

"Sometimes I wonder if she's real or a figment of my imagination," Karen said after the door closed silently.

"I know. Nobody should be that quiet. Or serene. It's kind of creepy."

"What's creepy is that she weighs ninety pounds soaking wet and works with cake all day. It's not fair." She stared at the door broodingly. "What is Vinyasa flow anyway?"

"Some kind of yoga, I think."

"Maybe I should take up yoga. Maybe I'd end up as thin as Laurel."

Chelsea shook her head. "Are you back to that again?"

"Did I ever leave it?"

"Someday you will meet a man who adores your curves."

"I should have been born in the era of Mae West and all those tiny, chubby pin-up girls." She put her hands on her ample hips. "Instead, I come of age when the ideal is a ten-foot-tall anorexic. It's not fair."

"I would think a lot of men would prefer a curvy woman to an elongated skeleton."

Karen thought of her and Dex on her desk and felt heat suffuse her face.

Chelsea was quick to pick up on it. "Oh, no. Look at you blushing and staring at the floor. Have you met such a man?"

"No. Not exactly." And she realized that her feelings about Dex were far too confusing to share with anyone. Instead she said, "That CPA e-mailed me. He said he enjoyed our coffee date."

"That's great, right?"

"Yes, I suppose. I didn't think it was a very exciting date though."

"Give the guy a chance. You said yourself he was nice."

"He was. You're right." And maybe a nice man was exactly what she needed to keep her thoughts off a certain architect. "I should suggest dinner or a movie or something."

"That's the spirit. And he's not the only single man in Philly, you know. Who else is out there?"

She glanced up and put a hand over her mouth. "I keep forgetting to check the Web site."

Unfortunately for her, when she got back to her office for her rescheduled meeting with Sophie, Dexter had come along. For some reason she'd assumed he'd have enough tact not to show. Seemed she'd been wrong. She refused to blush when she met Dex's knowing gaze.

"Sophie, it's nice to see you again. What did you think of the bridal salons I suggested?"

"Fantastic. I found my dress. Look, I brought you

a picture," the woman gushed pulling out her digital camera. She'd chosen a perfect dress for her figure. Sleek and simple.

"Very classy," Karen said approvingly. "And for the bridesmaids?"

"I went with blue. It's Andrew's favorite color and he's not here to help choose anything, so at least I'm keeping him in mind."

"That's nice. And it's a good blue for a winter wedding." She consulted her notes. "Let's see, you're getting married at your aunt's house in mid February."

"Closest Saturday to Valentine's Day we could find."

"That's sweet," she said in her professional tone, controlling her gag reflex with an effort. "In my experience the men don't get too involved in the wedding details."

"Except for Dexter here. I don't know what I'd have done without him."

She sent him a thin smile and he responded with a wink. Suddenly he rose. "I've been meaning to tell you how much I like this desk, Karen," he said, walking toward it, standing in the very spot he'd stood when she'd so wantonly let herself be carried away by lust.

Heat suffused every inch of her body from her toes to the roots of her hair. She watched, unable to think of a thing to say as he ran his hands along the edge of the curved wood, caressing the grain the way he'd caressed her skin. "It's a lovely piece. Classy." He leaned against it. "Seems sturdy, too."

He must know it was since it had held up under the strain of them having sex on it.

"I didn't know you were interested in antiques, Dex," Sophie said, thankfully looking at the desk and not at

Karen who was forcing her blush down. The curse of being a redhead.

"I like classics," he said.

"Well, we all do," Karen interjected. "And I think your dress is absolutely classic. Now, I was talking to the florist this morning about you. I know you were keen on a garden theme even though we'll need to be indoors. He's a genius. He's suggesting pots of forced blooms and he wonders if you want to think about a four-seasons garden. His idea is that love is eternal, like an ever-blooming garden."

"Oh, what a fantastic idea. I love that," Sophie exclaimed. "And do you think he could include a few Italian plants since Andrew's family is Italian and he's been spending so much time in Italy?"

"I'll make a note of it," Karen said. "If you like the idea, he'll draw something up for you to look at."

Dexter didn't say much more during the meeting, but he didn't seem able to keep his hands off her desk.

She could barely concentrate. And the fact that Dexter knew exactly what he was doing to her, only made her more furious.

9

CHELSEA CAME INTO Karen's office with the spinach salad she hadn't had time to pick up and a formidable looking woman in a power suit and a riot of black curls framing a face dominated by big blue eyes and a square, "don't make me hit you" jaw.

"Do you have a minute if I bribe you with food?" Chelsea asked.

"Of course. Not that I consider salad food."

"You should have let me pack you a dessert."

"I don't want to talk about it."

Chelsea shot her a frustrated glance that suggested she'd soon be hearing some story about how fat was the new thin. But for now they weren't alone so she figured she was safe.

"This is David's sister, Sarah. She's getting married."

"Congratulations." Karen smiled politely but it was hard to hold herself back from outright laughing. Most brides came in looking excited, or nervous or blissed out on love.

Sarah seemed irritated about her impending bridalhood.

"Thanks. I'll be honest. I don't have a lot of time to plan a wedding, I've got a busy law practice, but I don't want a lot of hearts and flowers. And I won't be wearing white."

Fortunately, Chelsea had warned her about Sarah. The woman was a classic type A, an aggressive up-and-coming divorce lawyer who'd fallen for a school guidance counselor and part-time yoga teacher. Karen loved opposites-attract couples, but she had a feeling this was going to be one of the weirder pairings that made her job so much fun.

"You can wear whatever you want," Karen assured her. "Though popular tradition that wearing white is a symbol of purity isn't correct. The Greeks wore white as a color of celebration."

"Really?"

"Mmm-hmm. But the Western white wedding gown was popularized when Queen Victoria wore white to her wedding. At the time, only rich women could afford a dress they'd never wear again. Now, of course, any bride can wear whatever she wants."

"That's interesting, but I'm still not wearing white."

"That's fine."

She wondered if she really wanted to work with someone whose every sentence sounded like a barked order.

She glanced at Chelsea, wondering how she felt getting stuck with this woman for a sister-in-law. If she and David ever actually got married.

But she was surprised yet again when Chelsea said,

"Sarah's been my best friend since I moved here when I was fourteen."

Sarah's face softened completely when she smiled, Karen noted with relief, which it did now, in an impish grin. "You only hung out with me cause you had the hots for my big brother."

"Not true." She opened the takeout container and handed Karen a fork. "Not completely true. Go ahead and eat, I know you're starving."

"Yeah, please, don't mind me," Sarah said.

"I can't take notes and eat at the same time," Karen argued.

"Look, I don't think you're going to need a lot of notes. You probably won't even agree to plan this crazy wedding."

Once more she sent Chelsea a puzzled glance.

"Why wouldn't I want to plan your wedding?"

Sarah assumed her irritated expression once more. "It was my boyfriend's idea. He wants to recreate our first date."

Now Karen understood the irritation. She was beginning to feel some herself.

"You two went skydiving?"

"No."

"Hang gliding? Spelunking? Snorkeling? Some activity that took place underground, undersea or in the air?"

Sarah's eyes grew round. "Undersea? Are you kidding me?"

"Nope. I'm planning a scuba wedding for next summer as we speak."

"And don't forget the circus wedding," Chelsea reminded her. "I told you, Karen can do anything. She's amazing."

"Well, I never wanted a spectacle. I want to spend my life with the guy and that's it. I must really love him to let him talk me into this."

"Maybe you should tell us what it is?"

Sarah slapped her forehead with her open hand. A modest diamond twinkled on her ring finger. "I'm a serious person. Hardworking. A divorce lawyer. I have a certain reputation around town for toughness and smarts." She put down her hand and stared at Karen. "If news of this gets around, I'll be a laughingstock." She glared.

But Karen was pretty tough, too, and also had a reputation to upkeep. She adopted Sarah's drilling gaze. "Where did you have your first date?"

"I must have been insane," she said, more to herself, Karen thought, than to anyone else in the room. "I must still be insane."

From imagining feats of derring-do, her mind moved to seedier possibilities. If they'd done something sexually kinky or engaged in some illegal activity on their first date then she really didn't want any part of it.

She was a little firmer this time when she asked, "There are some weddings I won't plan. Where did he take you on your first date?"

As though admitting a terrible secret the woman said, "The zoo."

Once again, Karen had to struggle not to laugh at her newest potential client. "The zoo? Here in Philadelphia?"

"Yes," came the sulky reply. "Mike is this weird alternative guy. He adopted a zoo animal as part of their conservation program and he took me to the zoo on our first date to meet little Mikey."

"I'm guessing this is an opposites-attract kind of relationship."

"Oh, you've got that right. I'm a classic Type A." Like Karen might not have figured that out yet. "Mike's all Zen about everything. Doesn't own a microwave, only has one clock in his house. He's a high-school counselor and he teaches yoga."

There was a beat of silence. "I'm guessing he's great in bed," Karen said before she could censor herself.

To her relief Sarah laughed, a husky, earthy laugh. "Oh, he is. It's the only reason I put up with him."

"Huh," her old friend said. "What she means is, he's the only guy who's ever put up with her."

That laugh came again. "True."

"Well, I can tell you that a wedding at the zoo is easy to arrange, it's a popular spot for weddings and if it means something to the two of you then you should do it."

She took a shaky breath that Karen suspected was more about the idea of getting married at all than about the venue. "All right, then. Let's do it."

Karen began to take notes. "And I'm sure you know that Chelsea is the best caterer in town."

"Totally."

"And Laurel will do you an amazing cake."

"I'm not having a cake with zoo animals on it," she protested. "It's bad enough getting married at the zoo without having a wedding cake that should be at a kids' birthday party."

"Laurel would never be so boring as to put a zoo animal on a cake. You can meet with her to discuss your needs."

"No, no. You do it. Honestly, I want to leave everything in your hands."

After that it was easy. Sarah was businesslike, knew how many people were coming, had chosen several possible dates in the summer and very clearly liked to delegate. To Karen, that made her close to a dream client.

"I am so excited," Chelsea said at one point, her eyes shining with emotion.

The usually tough Sarah softened immediately. She leaned over to grip Chelsea's hand. "Me, too. And when you and David get married, we won't only be best friends. We'll be sisters."

Would they? Karen couldn't help but wonder.

Chelsea seemed genuinely excited about seeing her best friend get married before she could drag the woman's older brother to the altar.

Not for the first time, Karen wondered what was wrong with David to keep an amazing woman like Chelsea waiting.

He'd almost lost her once through his own stupidity. Karen was worried he was about to repeat his mistake.

Mistakes. There seemed to be a lot of those in the air.

Chelsea's cell phone rang and, after checking the call display, she backed out of the room. "It's Anton. I'd better get back. Come visit me when you're done with Karen," she said to Sarah, and with a wave she was gone.

It didn't take long for Karen to extract all the information she needed for now. Then, on a hunch, she said, "Can I ask your professional opinion about something?"

"Sure. I can't give free legal advice, but I can give you information if I've got it."

The second Sarah had mentioned being a divorce lawyer, she'd felt the urge to ask her a couple of questions. But now she had the woman's attention, she wasn't sure how to begin. Finally, she plunged in.

"In your experience, how many men who cheat on their wives claim to be innocent?"

Sudden sympathy clouded the clear eyes. "Ninety-five percent. You can catch them with a naked woman in bed and their pants around their ankles and they'll still say—" here she shook her index finger in Karen's direction and lowered her voice "—I did not have sexual relations with that woman."

Karen nodded, sadly. "That's what I thought."

_10_

OKAY, KAREN DECIDED, at the end of the day, when, no matter how busy she'd been, she'd always found time to relive the things she and Dexter had done on her desktop.

Enough was enough. Dexter was a player, a Casanova, a Lothario. Of course he was great in bed, he'd had plenty of experience. Some of it, she had to remind herself, while they were married. She'd begun to feel a spark of hope that maybe she'd been wrong about him, but Sarah the divorce lawyer had pretty much killed that notion.

Just because she felt a connection didn't mean there was one.

She was so angry with herself for falling like a ton of bricks the minute he came onto her. She'd assumed that once he'd had her again he'd disappear, but he'd shown up at Sophie's planning meeting, teasing her about that desk. He seemed still to be sniffing around her.

If she didn't care about him even after all this time maybe she could go along with it, have a fling with her ex. She wouldn't be the first woman ever to do so. But she'd worked long and hard to rebuild her self-esteem after it had been shattered by the man she'd loved and she wasn't about to compromise her hard-won peace again. Not for some cheap sex and a few orgasms, intense though they might be.

Gritting her teeth, she made a date with her laptop. She'd spend the evening going through all the listings at Plenty of Phillys. She had some messages to answer, some new profiles to check out.

When she got home that night, after a punishing thirty minutes at Curves, she zapped a low-cal dinner in the microwave which tasted so uninteresting it felt like a complete waste of four hundred calories, then showered and decided that if she was going to do this online dating thing then she'd better put a little effort into it.

Wrapping her towel around her she padded into her bedroom. She'd bought the town house after her marriage ended and she'd gone out of her way to make her bedroom as feminine as possible. Decorated in soft pinks and creams with a raw silk bedspread and white-and-gold French Provincial furniture, the room all but sported a No Boys Allowed sign on the door.

She opened her closet and tried to work out what one wore to go trolling for men using the Internet. She finally decided on a black cashmere V-neck sweater and black stretch exercise pants that were the most comfortable slacks she'd ever owned.

She let her hair dry naturally, curling down her back as it did when she didn't ruthlessly straighten and style it, and then she poured herself a glass of wine and logged onto the dating site.

There were a couple of men who'd sent her expressions of interest but she didn't like the appearance of either of them. Then she decided she'd better look around and see if anyone in her general age range caught her interest. She was clicking listlessly through the offerings when her doorbell rang.

Her video display showed her Dexter waiting at her front door with all the assurance of a man who knows he's welcome.

Wrong.

She ignored him and padded back to her couch.

Her cell phone rang.

She picked it up. "Yes?"

"I know you're home," said the all-too-familiar voice. "I checked. Your car's in your spot."

"Hmm, could there be a reason why I might be home and not answering my door? Oh, wait, there is. I don't want to see you."

"I came to say goodbye."

"Goodbye?" she blurted, much too fast for someone who didn't want to see the man. She couldn't believe he was leaving.

"I have to go back to New York for a couple of weeks, but I'll be back."

"Oh." Fine. It was fine. She'd managed without him for years, she didn't need him now.

"Could I come in? I want to talk to you."

Reluctantly, she let him in. Was he going to try to seduce her? One for the road? She couldn't believe he'd be that crass, and yet she must have a few crass bones in her body too for the idea didn't repel her. Maybe he was bad for her in a whole bunch of ways, but the sex was still so good it wasn't fair.

However, he didn't rush in and jump her. Instead, after he'd come in and removed his coat and shoes, he shoved his hands in the pocket of his jeans and seemed a little unsure of himself. In her feminine space, he seemed more than usually masculine and since she wasn't wearing her heels he towered above her.

"Would you like to sit down?"

"Yeah. Sure."

"Can I get you something? Some wine?"

"If it's open."

She went into her kitchen and poured him a glass.

Her body felt tingly and the scent of her body lotion rose as her skin heated from the images flashing through her brain. Good thing she'd showered and freshened up, she thought even as she tried to remind herself of all the reasons why having sex with the hottie in her living room was a bad, bad idea.

When she'd run out of lecture, she walked back in to find him sitting, not where she'd left him, but in her chair. And, horror of horrors, he was staring at her laptop screen with undisguised fascination.

He glanced up. "Are you kidding me? Online dating?"

"What's wrong with online dating?"

"Nothing, I guess. I thought…" He seemed to run out of steam and she didn't press him to finish his sentence. Instead she handed him the wine.

With a brief word of thanks, he took a sip and then put the glass down so he could devote his full attention to her computer. How could she have been so stupid as to have left the thing open for him to find?

Of course, anyone with any integrity wouldn't have snooped. But as she well knew, integrity wasn't Dexter's strong suit. If she made a big deal about it, he'd only laugh at her, so she decided to humor him. If he wanted to mock her and her efforts to find a nice guy, then that was his problem.

She steeled herself while he continued reading. Until she couldn't stand it anymore. "Why are you reading the profiles of single men in the city?"

"I'm not. I'm reading yours."

She rose. Enough already. She'd get that computer out of his hands if she had to wrestle him to the ground for it.

Finally he glanced up and shook his head. "I can't believe your profile. You missed all the best things about yourself."

That wasn't at all what she'd expected and he didn't appear to be teasing. She faltered. Puzzled. "Why do you say that?"

His expression was impossible to read. "Because no one knows you the way I do."

11

"ARE YOU SUGGESTING I should get you to write my online dating profile?" she asked, wondering if she could have misunderstood him.

"Why not?"

"Because you're my ex-husband. It seems a little unorthodox."

"Like I said, nobody knows you better, or knows all your good qualities better than I do." He grinned at her. "Of course, I know all your not-so-good qualities, too, but I'll keep those to myself."

"This seems like a really bad idea."

"Come on, let me take a crack at it. If you don't like what I write, you can delete it."

Intrigued in spite of her better judgment, she said, "What would you say?"

She had her legs curled under her, sitting in a corner of the couch. He picked up the laptop and brought it over, sitting beside her. His thighs brushed her toes and she felt a zing of connection from nothing more than the denim warmed by his body heat shifting against her foot.

He didn't move away.

And she didn't pull her foot out of the way.

He typed. She was certain he was correcting her height, knocking her down to size, but when she couldn't stand hearing the tap-tap-tap of keys, and watching the concentration on his face as he typed, she finally leaned over to check his progress.

What he wrote was, To know Karen you have to be patient. She's outgoing and funny, has a laugh that makes people join in and the minute you meet her you feel like you've known her forever. His fingers paused and she waited, silent, until they resumed. But to know the real Karen, the one behind the fun-loving social creature, takes work. She doesn't show her true self to many people, but it's worth waiting for. She's gorgeous, with clear blue-green eyes that make you think you're on the bottom of the ocean.

"Oh, Dex," she whispered, but he ignored the interruption.

Her skin's Irish fair, with a few freckles that remind you of the kid inside her. Her skin tastes like rain-washed apples, and she smells like cherry blossoms.

"Do I?" she murmured. It was like reading a love letter while it was being written, both romantic and the sexiest thing she'd ever seen. Those long artistic architect's fingers moved with precision over the keys, barely hesitating, as though all this had been composed in his mind and it was a simple matter to type it all out.

"You do. Stop interrupting." He thought for a moment and continued.

Her hair is a rich red, it's long and curly, thick

enough that you could wrap it around your hands like rope, but when she's making love to you, looking up with those big clear bottom-of-the-ocean eyes, her hair seems to catch fire, sparking flame. Hot and cold. Cold and hot.

"I'm not," she said, feeling breathless.

"You are."

And when she's naked her body is a glory. Breasts so rich and full you can fill your hands with them. But go carefully, for they are sensitive to the touch.

She made a tiny sound in the back of her throat.

He took one hand off the keyboard, as though he were pausing to think, and ran it across her nipples, already pebbled inside her cashmere sweater. She sighed, rippling her body against him like a cat desperate for affection.

He turned his head, looking down at her with lust blazing in his eyes. She didn't even think, simply pushed her computer off his lap and onto the couch, and then threw herself at him.

He caught her against him, crushing his mouth to hers, shoving his hands into the curling mass of hair tumbling around them, and began giving her what she needed.

Off came her sweater. Underneath it, she wore a sexy black camisole and, since she hadn't expected company and had wanted to feel at her sexiest, she wore no bra.

He groaned when he realized this, running his hands over her, squeezing her breasts in the way he knew she liked, firm but not too hard, and never squeezing the nipples, which were exquisitely sensitive.

Instead he kissed them, suckled them, bringing her

close to climax. She used to be embarrassed by how responsive her nipples were, but she'd learned to accept the easy pleasure. She leaned back, loving the feelings coursing through her body and the murmured appreciation from this man.

But she didn't want this to be a quickie, like the desktop escapade. She wanted time to enjoy him, especially if he was going to be gone for a few weeks. This was her chance to savor him, and then she could figure out what she was going to do about her inconvenient passion once he was out of state.

So she rose, took his hand and pulled him toward her bedroom. She flipped on the bedside lamps, which cast a muted pink glow over everything. Except Dex, who somehow still managed to look masculine and commanding.

She wanted to see all of him, enjoy every inch of his body, so she slowly undressed him, pulling off his sweater, the T-shirt he wore beneath it.

"I see you still work out," she murmured, running her lips over the muscular ridges of his belly.

The pale slash of an appendectomy scar, an old and nearly forgotten friend, drew her tongue and he sucked in his breath as she traced the line, something she'd done hundreds of times when he'd belonged to her. Moved by the memory, she suspected, as she was.

He was so familiar to her. His legs with the freckles above the knees, that ridiculous tattoo on his left shoulder he'd got on a drunken college trip to Thailand. He claimed he'd asked for an eagle and somehow either in a bad translation or a lack of artistic talent on the part of the tattoo artist, he'd ended up with a rooster on his back.

Which always made her smile. It was a reminder that

her ex-husband might be competent at business and brilliant at design, but he could be crazy and unpredictable and just as stupid as the next person.

"I see you still have Millie." And who but she would have named a rooster Millie?

He smiled at her, all dark eyes and simmering sexuality. "Do you know how much it costs to get a tattoo removed?"

She laughed at him, running her hands up and down his smooth, muscular back. "You've got lots of money. You're just a weenie about pain."

He grabbed her wrist and pulled her down beside him on the bed until they were in easy kissing distance. "You know me too well." He kissed her. "Which has some advantages."

"Such as?"

He grinned at her wickedly. "You know exactly what I like in bed."

And the truth was he knew the same about her. As he pulled her even closer and began playing with her body, and she began playing with his, she knew precisely what he meant.

Just touching him, feeling his skin warm under her hands, hearing from his whispered encouragement how much he enjoyed her own response got her hot, hotter, and finally too hot to hold. He'd always been able to gauge her response and pace himself accordingly so she had the bone-deep pleasure of feeling orgasm begin to swamp her and then feeling his pleasure double hers. It was the ultimate excitement and she'd never found it before or since.

But once the first round was over, and their urgent need slaked, they began to play, rolling and teasing, laughing and groping until the play turned serious, and they were making love once more.

"I can't keep up with you," he groaned, his body slick with sweat, his breathing ragged. "You are the most insatiable woman I've ever known. But you've worn me out. I need fuel." He slapped her rump playfully and rolled out of bed as gorgeous as she remembered. If anything his body had improved. It was so unfair.

"What have you got to eat?"

"Nothing. I ate earlier."

He yawned, still naked, like it was no big deal and then he headed for her kitchen. "Any leftovers?"

"No." She didn't want to tell him she'd stuck a frozen diet entrée in the microwave. It seemed so lonely somehow.

But Dexter seemed to think he had the right to entertain himself in her kitchen. Maybe he felt like he could still open her cupboards and fridge as though they were still married.

Because she had to find her robe and slip it on, plus find slippers and run a brush through the red tangle that used to be her hair, by the time she got to the kitchen, naked Dex was standing with his head in the freezer section of her fridge.

He turned to her with a look of disgust. "What is all this diet crap?"

"In case you hadn't noticed, I've put on a few pounds."

"No. You haven't." He shook his head and shut the door with the plastic thunk of a freezer that prefers to keep its secrets. "No wonder you're always in a pissy mood. You don't eat." He went for his coat and for a sad, sick moment she thought he was leaving, but he emerged with his BlackBerry. A couple of clicks and he was dialing.

"Who are you calling?"

"Chinese. Found a great delivery place."

"Not Chinese," she almost shouted.

With a puzzled expression he ended the call before it completed. "You always used to love Chinese."

"I still do," she moaned. "But I've used up all my calories today. I cannot watch you eat and not dig in."

"You need to quit this diet craziness, you hear me? You look fantastic. Even better naked than I remember." He grinned at her. "And I've got a very visual memory. It's an architect thing."

The thought of him comparing today's naked body with that of five years ago was enough to send her into the bathroom to slam the door and lock herself in until he was gone. "You're lying."

He shook his head and pressed redial. She heard him ordering all of her favorite foods and wondered if any woman would blame her if she killed the man by plunging chopsticks into his heart. So long as the jury was packed with women on diets, she knew no one would find her guilty.

While they waited for the food to arrive, he poured them another glass of the wine and pulled his jeans on.

They sat together, chatting, almost like old times.

"Tell me about your project," she asked.

"I'm excited about this one. The original building is a perfect example of classical revival architecture. The Stockard was built in the 1920s as the headquarters for a trading company, then converted to a bank and then a law firm. Our challenge is to transform The Stockard into a twenty-four-story mixed-use building with office, retail and luxury residential." He took a sip of wine and she knew he was picturing the project. "They'd already agreed to preserve the exterior façade and mezzanine, where most of the original historic details still exist. But we had to convince them that green building was the way to go. And we did."

"Congratulations," she said, knowing that Dex, with his passion and vision, was hard to resist.

"Thanks. We're mixing smart design with the original architectural detailing. Retail at street level, a couple of floors of offices and a separate entrance leads to top of the line condos. I love mixing old and new."

She smiled at his excitement. "It sounds amazing."

"It will be. I might buy one of the condo units." He shrugged. "See how they turn out."

She was surprised and she knew it showed on her face. "You'd move back to Philly?"

He flicked her a glance. "I don't know. Maybe. Or if I keep doing a lot of work here it might make sense to keep a place. I haven't decided yet."

She didn't know what she'd have said, wasn't even sure what she thought of the idea of him spending enough time in the city to keep a home here, when the doorbell sounded.

"Get the plates, will you?" he said, as he jogged down the stairs to answer the door.

"Plate. One," she muttered, even as she licked her lips in anticipation.

He jogged back in with a shallow box containing far too many takeout containers.

"What did you buy? Everything on the menu?"

"Sex makes me hungry. You know that." He plopped the box on the counter and flipped open a carton. Waved the thing under her nose. "Makes you hungry, too. Don't think I've forgotten."

"Oh, I am a weak, weak woman, and you are an evil, evil man," she said as she reached inside the container for a crispy chunk of ginger beef and popped it in her mouth where the spicy flavor exploded on her tongue.

From that moment she was lost.

They talked, they ate, and when she tried to stop, claiming she'd had enough, he started feeding her little pieces with his own chopsticks. When he dropped a fat, juicy prawn before it reached her mouth, so it slid down her chest, and then he went after it with his mouth, she laughed. "You did that on purpose."

"Maybe." He leaned forward and undid her robe.

"No," she cried, trying to pull the lapels back together.

"Let me look. You are so beautiful."

"After I lose five pounds."

"You're crazy, you know that?"

She shook her head at him.

He got a cunning look in his eye, one she knew well, and that stirred her blood. "What are you planning?"

"Maybe just a little peek."

She laughed, but the light in here was so bright. "You've already seen everything there is to see."

"Come on. I like to look at you."

But she let him ease open one side of her housecoat. Revealing one plump breast, the nipple already as round as a blueberry.

He glanced up at her, then back at her breast. "I haven't had dessert."

"Have a fortune cookie."

He reached for his chopsticks. "I have a better idea."

12

"Oh, no," she said, seeing where he was going. "Not the plum sauce." But she was already giggling.

He opened the little cello pack of prepared plum sauce, squeezed some out and painted her nipple with sauce. It felt sticky and cool and when she glanced down her nipple glistened.

To her shock, Dex took his chopsticks and snagged her nipple between them. "What are you…"

He lifted the plump flesh carefully toward his mouth, lowering his head until he could lick plum sauce off the end of her nipple. The sensation was intense: she felt the pressure of the wooden sticks, not squeezing tight, he'd never hurt her, but holding her, as though she were a morsel of food to be offered to his mouth. And then, beside the rigidity of the wood, clamping lightly, came the warm, wet caress of his tongue on her sensitive skin swirling the slick sauce around until she felt herself beginning to melt.

She didn't even try to protest when he pushed her robe away from her other side and proceeded to squeeze more plum sauce, take her other nipple between chopsticks. Lick and suck her halfway to oblivion.

Her robe was gone. Fallen away, and she didn't care that it was probably going to be ruined. He trailed plum sauce down her body in unpredictable patterns, following with his tongue.

When he hit her belly, she felt herself growing heavy and liquid with desire as she sat, sprawled on one of her designer kitchen stools.

"Now," he murmured, "I wonder where else I could use chopsticks."

"Oh, no, I—"

But he was already slipping her legs apart, and she was offering herself up like a banquet on a Lazy Susan. She watched through heavy lids as he parted her folds, exposing her clit which had no need of plum sauce to glisten.

He came slowly toward her with the chopsticks and she began to tremble.

She could pull away, shut her legs and close up shop, but she didn't. She watched. Everything about her was plump, including her intimate parts and when he took that most sensitive of her parts gently, ensnaring the root with the chopsticks, she thought she might fall onto the floor so wildly did the sensation rock her.

A strange sound, not moan or sigh, but some combination of both slipped from her mouth. He took the plum sauce, squeezed a dab onto her hot, aching clit. Then he began to lick it off, unbelievably gently because he knew how sensitive she was, how close.

Torture. It was torture. The most amazing, incredible, delicious torture. He wouldn't let her come. Controlled her as though her body was his, her response his to order.

Those hard, rigid sticks held her in place and that soft, mobile mouth made love to only that one spot.

Slowly.

Delicately.

Exquisitely.

She had her arms stretched out, hanging on to the cold granite countertop, it was the only way she could remain still. But nothing could stop the crazy sounds coming from her throat.

She thought she'd die of pleasure. It would go on forever and she'd never achieve release.

Then, as though he knew she couldn't take any more, he increased the speed of his movement, upped the pressure slightly and with a wild bucking cry, she exploded in his mouth.

"I need you…in me…NOW!" she yelled, but he was already stepping between her legs, already there, and as he thrust home, she cried out again.

MORNING LIGHT DAPPLED HER BODY as Karen stretched luxuriously, every cell in her body singing the "Hallelujah Chorus." The gesture pushed her breasts up and Dexter leaned over to kiss them, his face all manly with emerging stubble.

"I didn't mean to spend the night," he said.

"I didn't mean to let you." This was all too intimate, too familiar. In a minute, he'd suggest they shower together, or she would, and then they'd drink coffee and share the paper. She'd kiss him goodbye and wish him a good day.

"I'd almost forgotten how good we are together," he murmured.

The memories of the night before made her smile with mingled pleasure mixed with mild embarrassment that she'd been like a sex-crazed maniac last night. "I'll never look at Chinese food the same way."

"I'm having those chopsticks bronzed."

He reached for her breast where the persistent tingling told her her nipples had reacted to the memories. Of course, since he was currently pressed up against her, she could feel that his body had also reacted to the memories of last night.

His mouth closed on her breast. "You still taste like plum sauce. We should take a shower together."

Yep, right on cue. As though they were still the happily married couple who had sex with their takeout and showered together in the morning. But they weren't...

Suddenly a wave of mingled grief and rage swamped her, the likes of which she hadn't experienced since they'd first split up.

If they were so bloody good together, why weren't they still married?

"Why?" she whispered, knowing he could hear the anguish in her voice.

He raised his head and leaning on one elbow, gazed down at her. "Why what?" She suspected he knew exactly what her question referred to, but she obliged him anyway by expanding her question.

"Why did you cheat on me if we were so good together?"

His fingers traced a pattern down her chest.

A rueful half smile lit his face. "It always comes back to that, doesn't it? Here's a question for you. Why were you so quick to jump to a conclusion that was insulting to both of us?"

An inarticulate squeal formed in her throat. She felt the hot wash of betrayal sting her skin. "I saw you. She was half naked in your arms."

"I know what you saw, I was there. What you didn't see was me having sex with another woman because it never happened. I had no idea how to handle a nightmare embarrassing situation. She was messed up and needy and drunk or high. What you saw wasn't me undressing her, it was my trying to get her dressed so I could find you and we could take her home."

But the image of betrayal was burned on her retina. She could describe every part of the image as though she were describing a scene as it unfolded. "She was kissing you. You had your arms around her and were unzipping her dress." The anger felt so fresh and raw she wanted to smack him. Wanted to reverse time to the moment he'd arrived yesterday so she could tell him to go away.

"I was trying to zip it up! I've told you a hundred times. And she plastered her mouth on mine while I was doing it. Believe me, I wasn't kissing her back."

"How can I believe you?" she cried, knowing with all her heart that she wished his words were true, but she'd been cheated on before. So had her mom and her sister. In her experience and that of most women in her life, men weren't to be trusted.

She remembered her father, how good-looking he'd been and how special she'd felt in his company. He'd traveled a lot on business and the house used to be kind of empty and depressing when he wasn't there. Her mother always seemed to be in a bad mood. It wasn't until she'd grown older, and he'd finally left the family for good, that she understood that there was a lot of pleasure mixed in with his business trips.

Men couldn't help it, her mother hypothesized after the divorce when Karen pelted her with questions. It was part of their genetic makeup to spread their seed as far and wide as possible. Nature or nurture, Karen had sworn to herself that no man would make a fool of her that way, and she'd stuck to her principles.

If she'd been stupid to marry a man who was as good-looking and charming as her father, at least she hadn't put up with years of lying and cheating like her mother had.

As much as it had hurt her, she'd dumped the lying, cheating scumbag as soon as he showed his true colors.

But oh, she'd had no idea that part of her would be destroyed.

She thought he looked a little sad as he said, "No one can answer that question but you."

"I even tried to talk to her, you know. After."

"Who?"

"The model."

"How did you find her? She didn't even have a last name."

"I can be very persistent." And in some still naive, hopeful part of her she'd wanted the woman to corroborate her husband's story.

"Wow. I can't believe you tracked her down."

Her eyes narrowed. "I don't hear you getting all excited about how she backed up your story."

"Because I'm not stupid. If she had, we wouldn't be here now. We'd still be married." He shook his head. "Actually, we probably wouldn't. Some other shadow would have frightened you away."

"You're right about one thing. She didn't corroborate your story."

He snorted. "So, you'd believe a drunk woman without a last name before you'd believe me."

"All she told me was that she couldn't remember

anything about that night. By the time I tracked her down she was in rehab."

"Great. Just great," he said. "That father of yours sure did a number on you."

"Don't you blame my father. He had nothing to do with this. The only mistake I made was in marrying a man just like him." She pulled the covers up so her breasts were no longer exposed.

He rolled to his back, putting distance between them. She felt cold without his arms around her. "The mistake you made was not believing you hadn't. It all comes down to trust."

"You hurt me."

"You hurt me, too." He'd never said those words to her before and as she turned to him, she saw that it was true. Whatever he'd done, at least he felt the loss of their marriage. She supposed that was something.

"Some days I wish I'd never met you."

"I should have made you go to marriage counseling with me," he said at the same moment.

"There was no point," she insisted.

He jabbed a finger toward the living room. "Do you think there's a perfect man in that computer storehouse out there? Some guy who won't ever come home late or go on business trips with attractive women? What are you going to do? Spend your life savings on private dicks and all your energy on suspicion?"

"No. No, I'm not. I believe there's a nice man out there who can be faithful."

"Do you?"

"Mmm-hmm. I won't set my sights so high this time."

He rolled over and got back up on his elbow so he could stare down into her face. "Come again?"

"I've done a lot of reading since we broke up. There are theories about what makes a successful relationship and one of them is that you should match up with people who are similar status to you." She shrugged. "So, really good-looking people should stick together and more homely people should go with homely ones. I was always so flattered when you took an interest in me, but I think in the end you're too good-looking. Too successful."

He blinked at her, his face darkening with anger. "That is the biggest load of bullshit I've ever heard," he argued, pulling himself up to sitting. "Setting aside the fact that I think you're beautiful, what does that say about me? In ten years, when you start to age, do I turn you in for a younger model? What about love? What about the old-fashioned idea of sticking together through thick and thin? Better and worse and all that?"

"I don't know."

"I don't know, either." He rolled out of bed, unconcerned that he was naked. Even though she was angry and confused she couldn't help but drink in her fill of that tall, buff body and wish things could have turned out differently.

He pulled on his clothes swiftly and efficiently and then walked over to where she sat in bed, watching him.

"Is this really about me being unfaithful or is it about you being insecure?"

"I'm not insecure, I'm realistic."

He made a dismissive sound. "Tell that to your mirror."

"I—"

"I didn't fall in love with a status symbol. I never thought you did, either. I think you're gorgeous, and successful. I like your curves. Did it ever occur to you that I wasn't the one who betrayed our marriage?"

"I don't have any idea what you're talking about. You can't make this my fault."

"I can't make you see reason." She thought he'd say more, then he clamped his mouth shut.

"I'll be back in a couple of weeks. Take care of yourself."

"You, too."

He kissed her swiftly. Rose and as he reached the door of her bedroom turned back. "Oh, and you might want to edit that profile before you post it."

13

DEX WAS GORGEOUS, sexy, dangerously good in bed and completely bad for her. Forget sex with Dex. She had to start over.

So after that fiasco she renewed her online efforts. Thursday she had a lunch date with a guy named Larry who spent the entire time talking about his ex-wife and what a bitch she was. It was so depressing she had a headache when she returned to the office.

Saturday evening she had drinks with Steve who admitted over his second martini that while his profile claimed he was divorced, he wasn't completely divorced.

"How close are you?" she asked.

Larry ran a hand through rapidly receding hair. "I can't upset her right now, she's moody. But as soon as I find my soul mate, I'm telling my wife right away."

She declined to stay for dinner.

When she reviewed her latest date with Dee the young woman said, "Okay, it's time for some advanced tips and hints."

"I'm ready."

"One." The young woman twirled a blond curl around her pencil. "At your age, it's borderline on whether a guy's been married or not, but if they get close to forty and they've never been married or had a significant relationship, that's a big red flag. Mommy issues? Can't commit? Do some investigation before you commit to anything."

Karen thought about Ron, the CPA who at thirty-seven had never been married. She suspected she'd already met one of those.

"Got it."

"Two. If a guy says he's divorced, when you e-mail him make sure—"

"Oh, I've got this one. First question I should be asking is how long they've been divorced."

Her dating mentor nodded. "And make sure they're living on their own."

"Huh?"

"Catholic divorce. It's where the wife lives on one level of the house and the ex lives on the other. With this bad economy, lots of couples are doing it, but I wouldn't go there."

"Right. That could be complicated."

"Kids is another issue."

"I like kids."

"I know you do. That's my point. If you're going to have kids, no offense, you don't have a lot of time to waste, so if a guy doesn't have any, you want to find out pretty soon if he's open to kids. And if he has some, find out if he sees them a lot. Best way to discover if a guy is going to be a good father is to see if he already is one."

"Wow. This is more like landing a great job than finding eternal love."

"Love won't last if you don't share basic goals and values," Dee informed her.

She was filled with affection for her assistant. "So young and so wise."

By paying more attention to the details in a profile she did manage to avoid a couple more disasters and no one jumped out at her as the potential father of the kids she'd better have quick according to Dee, before she ended up barren as well as alone.

The following Wednesday, against her better judgment, she went to the movies with Ron. Who probably had mommy issues, possibly also commitment phobia. But he was a nice man and she didn't really like her own company right now. Afterward, they stopped at a coffee shop and found, as they had before, that if they talked about their businesses, they got on fine. But on the personal front, they didn't have much in common.

"Is this how most of your dates go?" she finally asked him.

He shook his head. "No. Most are much, much worse."

To her surprise she burst out laughing. "So you're saying this is bad?"

He immediately tried to reassure her that they weren't bad. He liked her a great deal and it was refreshing to be able to spend time with someone who enjoyed discussing business.

She reached out and touched his hand, which was cool and dry. "But there's no spark, is there?"

The gray eyes she liked so much lifted to hers. "No."

She sipped her coffee, thinking she'd miss this quiet, unassuming man who was so easy to talk to and who she'd never imagine getting caught with a half dressed woman on his arm. "I'll miss you."

"I hope we can still see each other. This can be a lonely city when you're not part of a couple. I'd like for us to stay friends." He shifted the sugar until it was exactly in line with the napkins. "At least until one of us starts seeing someone seriously."

She was oddly flattered. "I don't have many male friends. I'd like that."

When they parted he kissed her cheek and she went home alone. Even though she'd changed the sheets after Dex left her, and that had been almost a week ago, she still couldn't seem to get the elusive scent of him out of her bed. She knew it was only her memory playing tricks on her, but oh, it had been a mistake to let him into her bed again.

She'd gone out and bought all new furniture after they split up and the first item she'd purchased had been that bed because she never wanted to sleep alone in the place they'd once shared so much.

Now he'd come and polluted her bed with his presence, and the room was thick with the memories of their night together, the passion, the heat, the searing intimacy.

Oh, she'd slept with a couple of men after her divorce, but not for a while now, mainly because no man had ever come close.

So she went back to planning joyous occasions for brides who didn't know what they were letting themselves in for, giving them the magical day that would seal their doom. Then she came home to a house that had never felt empty until Dexter forever stamped his presence onto it.

Another week and one more dismal date with a guy

who claimed to be a marathon runner, a millionaire investor and a philanthropist. Ten minutes in his company told her he was a compulsive liar since he was overweight, smoked, seemed to think Dow Jones was a baseball pitcher, and sneered at a sad-looking street person.

Would you like to go to dinner tonight? Ron asked her. They had fallen into the habit of e-mailing a few times a week and she enjoyed a certain quiet humor about him, plus the fact that he was pretty much who he said he was.

She was busy with meetings and a bridal show, plus she had a meeting with Sophie Vanderhooven scheduled for the next morning. Sophie had said Dex would probably be at the meeting, which meant he would probably drop by her place since they seemed to have fallen into some kind of ex-with-benefits scenario.

Of course it was a bad idea to sleep with her ex. But ice cream and chocolate bars were bad ideas, too, and she was just as addicted.

I think I'd better— She stopped herself with a start before turning down this nice, uncomplicated single man in order to sit home in case her cheating ex should decide to drop by for sex. What was she doing?

She resumed typing. I think I'd better start inviting you places since you always seem to do all the work. But yes, I'd love to.

Do you like Chinese food?

Heat washed over her. She e-mailed back. No food that involves chopsticks.

Then he mentioned a popular American eatery downtown, which could have no awkward memories attached to it. She agreed.

I'll pick you up at seven.

Perfect. He was the kind of man who treated her like a date even though they were friends which was fine with her. It was nice not to have to drive in heels and figure out parking.

He was prompt as always, but she was ready when he arrived.

Over dinner she finally told him that she might be interested in his services and described a few accounting muddles.

He nodded. "I think I might be able to help you. What I should do is give you a couple of references of other customers so you can get a sense of my work."

Once dinner was over he drove her correctly home. It was only ten o'clock and she got the feeling that he was in no hurry to head to his lonely house. "Would you like to come in for coffee?" She hesitated, then clarified, "And I do mean coffee."

"Do you have decaf?"

"Of course."

"Then I'd like to."

Since he was more worried about caffeine than her hot bod she didn't fret about him getting the wrong idea about her invitation. While she went into the kitchen to make the coffee, he settled himself in her living room with the day's newspaper.

When she returned, he politely folded the paper and accepted his coffee.

"Can I ask you something?" she asked.

"Of course."

"Do you really think there's someone out there for you? A soul mate if you like?"

Ron pondered the question, the way she found he

tended to ponder most inquiries. "I think it would be sad to live the rest of my life alone," he said at last. "I have Beth, of course."

"Beth?"

"My new golden retriever."

"Oh."

"I'll be picking her up Thursday. She's a pup. Would you like to see a picture?"

"Of course I would."

He pulled out his wallet and showed her a truly adorable puppy that she could tell from the snap was all bounce and bubble.

"But I'd like to have a family and someone to come home to. I don't think I'm meant to live alone."

"I can understand that."

He crossed his ankles neatly in front of him and frowned down at them. The light from a table lamp glimmered on his glasses. "I was never the guy all the girls went crazy over. I suppose I keep hoping that someday I'll meet a nice woman who doesn't need to be dazzled, but is willing to settle down with a very average, reliable man. I realized years ago that I was never going to set the world on fire. But I'm a good accountant and I think I'd be a good husband and father."

She found herself warming to his honesty. "I think you'd make a wonderful husband."

"What about you?"

She made a face. "I found my soul mate. Didn't work out quite the way I planned."

"I'm sorry."

"Oh, well. At least I found out while I'm still young enough to try again. But I seem to keep meeting the most horrible men."

"I'm sure the women are worse."

She reviewed her brief dating history. "Couldn't be."

"I had a kleptomaniac who stole all the cutlery off the table when we had dinner, and then lifted the tip off the table. It wasn't until I realized my credit card was missing and went back to the restaurant that I found out what she was like."

"Oh, no," she cried in ready sympathy. "Did you get your card back?"

"Yes. Fortunately I cancelled the card before she could do much damage." He sent her a wry grin. "But I can never show my face in that restaurant again."

While they chatted companionably over coffee, and shared dating disasters, she discovered what she'd begun to suspect, that apart from his years away at college, he'd lived with his widowed mother until she died and still occupied his childhood home.

"Have you thought of moving?"

"Why would I? It's a nice solid home in a good area of town. No, I plan to stay."

"I think we're both stuck in the past a little bit. Maybe we simply need to shake things up a bit. We could move." She placed her empty coffee cup on the table in front of the couch.

"But I don't want to move."

She glanced around her town house. "I don't want to move, either."

He put down his own cup. "I should go." But the way he said it she felt that he didn't relish going home to an empty house just yet.

"I was going to watch the late show, do you want to join me?"

"Yes." He took off his jacket and settled beside her on the couch. It was nice to have the company, she realized. Nice to relax and not have to talk after the stress

Get 2 Books FREE!

Harlequin® Books,
publisher of women's fiction,
presents

GET 2 BOOKS

We'd like to send you two *Harlequin® Blaze™* novels absolutely free.
Accepting them puts you under no obligation to purchase any more books.

HOW TO GET YOUR
2 FREE BOOKS AND 2 FREE GIFTS

1. Return the reply card today, and we'll send you two *Harlequin Blaze* novels, absolutely free! We'll even pay the postage!

2. Accepting free books places you under no obligation to buy anything, ever. Whatever you decide, the free books and gifts are yours to keep, free!

3. We hope that after receiving your free books you'll want to remain a subscriber, but the choice is yours—to continue or cancel, any time at all!

EXTRA BONUS

You'll also get two free mystery gifts! (worth about $10)

FREE!

of the past few days. She'd been knocking herself out putting on back-to-back weddings and then trying to get ready for an upcoming bridal show, plus there was the whole Dexter situation. He either kept her awake all night in passion or in trying to figure out what she was going to do about him.

She yawned, hugely, tried to concentrate on what Jimmy Fallon was saying. After the commercial break he was going to interview a young actress about an upcoming movie.

But she never saw the interview. Before the opening monologue was over, she was sound asleep.

SUN STREAMING IN HER WINDOW woke Karen. She blinked, slowly, wondering where she was and what was different from most mornings.

With a start, she realized she was dressed in last night's clothes and the warm weight resting against her wasn't Dexter.

It was Ron.

Sound asleep and looking rather forlorn, he had an arm thrown around her while her head rested on his shoulder.

"Ow," she said, raising her head and trying to rub the stiffness from her neck.

Either her speaking or moving woke Ron, who blinked owlishly a few times and glanced around.

"Oh," he said, when his puzzled gaze encountered hers. "I guess we fell asleep."

"I guess so."

She didn't know which of them was more embarrassed, as they moved to opposite sides of the couch. She rose, pulling her skirt into place as she did so. "Would you like some coffee?"

"Oh, uh." He cleared his throat, put on the glasses that had fallen onto the floor, glanced at his watch. "No, thank you. I've got to get back to my place and get ready for the day. I'd better be going."

"All right. Well." She had no idea what to say. "Thanks for last night."

He stood up and seeing him so rumpled made her realize what a meticulous dresser he usually was. He looked exactly like a man who'd slept in his clothes. His hair was up on one side and his sweater askew. "I had a nice time, too. I'm sorry that I fell asleep."

This was the most ridiculous situation. In spite of herself she laughed. "I won't tell if you don't."

He smiled perfunctorily, slipping his feet into his loafers. "No. I won't be telling anyone." He rubbed at his stubbled face. "Sometimes, it gets lonely. Living alone."

"I know. Look, I'm putting on coffee anyway. You should at least have coffee."

He shook his head. "Perhaps I could use the bathroom before I leave?"

"Of course."

She started coffee and then he appeared in the kitchen. He'd obviously washed his face since the hair above his forehead was damp. A droplet of water clung to one eyelash. He looked oddly adorable and she felt more like his mother than a date as she led him to the front door once he'd refused once more to stay for coffee.

"Why don't you come to my office tomorrow? I could show you around and then show you my books which are, I admit, a bit of a mess."

"Certainly. I could do that."

"I'll even buy you lunch. You haven't lived until you've tried Chelsea Hammond's lasagna."

"I'll see you tomorrow, then."

She opened the door as he leaned in to kiss her cheek.

"Good morning," a cheerful male voice boomed out from the other side of the open doorway.

Ron's lips hadn't even reached her cheek before darting off again.

Oh, horror of horrors. If there was one person in all the world she wouldn't have wanted to know about her little escapade, it would have to be the man currently striding up her front walk with a box in his arms. She said the first thing she thought of. "What are you doing here?"

"Delivering a bridesmaid gown." He nodded to the man standing awkwardly by her side. "Not for me, you understand."

"Of course."

She and Ron stood rooted foolishly in her front doorway. The day was overcast and cold. A light frost covered the ground. Dexter removed one of his driving gloves and held out his hand to Ron. "Dexter Crane, delivery boy."

Automatically, the men shook hands. "Ron Turgison, CPA," the befuddled man beside her replied.

"Ah, a good man to have around."

Another beat passed. Finally, she reached for the box Dex was holding and at the same time Ron said, "Well, goodbye. I'll call you."

He left and Dexter walked into her house without an invitation. "Now that's nice. A man should always call after he spends the night at a woman's place. Good manners."

"Would you drop the Cary Grant act?" She put her head in the hand that wasn't holding the box. "This is so not what it looks like."

"No?" Dexter said mildly. "It looked pretty clear to me."

The sheer enormity of trying to explain what had just happened was too much for an uncaffeinated woman to handle. "I need coffee. Before I speak, I need coffee."

He followed her.

When she reached the living room she discovered the television was still on. She'd somehow slept through an entire night of late-night, even later-night, after-late, late shows and infomercials and early, early, early shows without ever waking. She put the dress box down and picked up the remote to snap off the TV.

She stomped into the kitchen and then snapped, "Why are you delivering things to my house at seven-thirty in the morning?"

"The slick answer is that Andrew surprised Sophie with a first-class plane ticket to Italy. She sends her apologies, she won't be able to make your meeting. However, she picked up a sample of the bridesmaid dress in New York for you to match flowers and things. Since I had to come back to Philly, she asked me to deliver the dress." He stuck both gloves in the pocket of his overcoat, slipped it off and laid it over the back of one of her kitchen chairs. It was too long and the gray wool bunched on the tile floor. "The honest answer of course is that I wanted to see you."

And she supposed he'd come early enough that they could indulge in a pre-work quickie. Except that he'd found another man leaving her house as he was arriving. What a mess.

She shouldn't be embarrassed. She was a single

woman. Why shouldn't she have men coming and going at all hours? But she did feel foolish. "I never should have slept with you again," she snapped.

"Pour the coffee. You're never at your best before the first cup."

"Stop reminding me that you know me so well."

"But I do," he said softly. He didn't sound irate or angry, but she could tell he was waiting for the explanation she'd promised him.

As she turned to pour coffee, she wished she were at least wearing her heels and didn't look as disheveled as she was certain a mirror would confirm. She poured two mugs of coffee, adding milk only to hers, milk and sugar to Dex's as she knew he liked it.

She pushed the mug at him and drank her own gratefully. Then she caught his gaze. If anything he was looking slightly amused.

"Let's sit down. I can't stand you towering above me."

They sat at her kitchen table since she didn't even want to think about what had happened when they'd sat side by side on the stools at her counter.

She said, "Ron's a guy I met online." She glanced up and then down at her coffee. "He's nice."

Still Dexter didn't say a word.

"We went out for dinner last night and then we came back here to watch the late show. I know it sounds unbelievable, but we both fell asleep watching TV. We'd just woken up when you got here." She traced her finger over the handle of her green pottery coffee mug. "I didn't sleep with him."

"Thank you for telling me," he said and sipped from his matching green mug. "You still make the best coffee of anyone I know. Maybe it's the beans. I should find out from you where you get them."

Coffee beans? He wanted to talk about coffee beans? What kind of emotional game playing was this?

"Dexter, I'm telling you the truth. I know it looks like Ron and I spent the night together—" She stopped, realizing they had in fact spent the night together. "I mean, had sex, but we didn't."

"Yes. You said that. I heard you."

Irritation, completely irrational but red-hot, geysered through her. "Fine. Don't believe me. I don't know why I bothered trying to explain anything. Forget it. Think whatever you want."

A hand, long-fingered and strong, came to rest on hers where it lay fisted on the tabletop. He squeezed her fingers, causing her to look up and meet his gaze. To her astonishment, he smiled at her, with warmth and humor. His hand felt warm and comforting enclosing her own.

"Here's the part where I get to give you a little lecture, for your own good, and you get to listen."

If it was anything about safe sex she was going to hit him over the head with her coffee mug, she decided, tensing.

"Maybe nine out of ten men would see a man with really bad bed-head leaving your house at seven-thirty in the morning and figure you'd spent the night doing more than watch Craig Ferguson—"

"Jimmy Fallon."

"Whoever. The point is, you told me you didn't sleep with him, and I believe you."

She glanced sharply up at him, having a hard time accepting that he was telling the truth. Her eyes narrowed. "Why?"

"Here's the really good part, so listen carefully." He leaned closer, and she saw that he'd shaved extra close this morning, and that his eyes were direct and honest. "I trust you."

"But—"

"That's it. I trust you. If you tell me you were annotating some obscure line in your taxes, or calculating your 401K contributions all night, I'll believe that, too."

She yanked her hand out from under his, no longer feeling comforted but smothered. "Oh, no. I'm not going to let you do this. You're trying to compare Ron leaving my house fully dressed to finding that woman half-naked and wound all over you? The two aren't even remotely similar."

He leaned back in his chair and raised his mug in a mock toast. "They are so similar that poetic justice is written all over this scenario." He slugged back another jolt of coffee. With a well-pleased expression on his too-handsome face, he rose. "Well, I've got a meeting at nine. I'd better get going. I'll see you around."

He walked out and she jumped to her feet to follow him.

"Don't you dare try and suggest that you're a better person than I am because the cases aren't remotely similar. You can say whatever you like but you knew from the first second that I hadn't had sex with Ron."

He'd reached the front door but he turned, laughter sparking in his eyes.

"Karma may be a bitch, but today she's my bitch."

14

WITH A DEFT TWIST of her wrist that she'd perfected over the years, Laurel created the pink icing petal of a rosebud just bursting into bloom. Sure, she could create any kind of cake she was asked for, but it was always reassuring to come back to tradition.

No one would believe her, so she never bothered to voice the thought, but she loved creating the traditional wedding cakes. This one was a perfect delight of white icing over three separate layers of traditional fruit cake, which she made herself from her Irish grandmother's recipe. The only color was provided by the pink roses which exactly matched the color of the bride's bouquet. She'd sourced a few extra roses from the florist and matched the color perfectly, adding darker shadings with a paintbrush.

Laurel loved her job. She'd always enjoyed baking and art growing up and had never realized she could put the two together in the perfect career until she landed a part-time job working in a bakery one summer.

She'd been hired to fry donuts, but when the do-nuts were done she was free to help whoever needed her. Sometimes she greased the bread pans, sometimes she washed gunked cooking pots in a deep stainless steel sink, but her favorite task was helping the cake decorators. An apt and eager pupil, she was soon learning everything she could about the art and science of cake making and decorating and before long she had certainly outstripped her mentor in originality if not technique.

Her cakes might have remained nothing more than a fun summer job if she hadn't been asked to make a wedding cake for a young couple who begged for something different. After asking them about their interests and discovering they were avid skateboarders, she created a skateboard park out of cake and icing, assuming at worst that she'd be fired and at best that she'd give the two getting married what they actually wanted.

She didn't get fired. She started getting orders of her own and, luckily, the senior cake decorator didn't seem to mind. In fact, she helped Laurel turn some of her crazier ideas into reality, teaching her how to perfect her fondant and how to add tensile strength to her icings.

At the end of high school, she'd gone to a baker's college and after working in New York for what was basically a wedding cake factory, she'd come home to Philly and started out on her own.

Meeting Karen the wedding planner and then Chelsea Hammond, the caterer, had been amazing. She didn't like selling herself, she loved to create cakes. By joining up with Karen and Chelsea, they did the selling and she did the baking and icing of fantasy to traditional cakes and everyone was happy.

In the big industrial kitchen where Chelsea's catering business was located, she had her own section. Originally, the idea had been for the two to share the kitchen but the truth was that Chelsea's business had grown so fast that she could well afford the space all to herself.

And Laurel was doing so well with her cakes, frankly shocked at the prices Karen and Chelsea charged for her creations, that she could have moved to a new place.

But she liked working here and Chelsea claimed that she was the kitchen muse so they'd worked out a deal where she paid much less than half the rent and enjoyed working in the busy kitchen. If the noise got too much, she could always slip the Panda earbuds into her ears and turn on her iPod, but she rarely did. She found that she worked best with the bustle of a busy kitchen surrounding her, the good-natured back and forth of the catering staff and the occasional rushes.

Today, however, there were no rush orders, it was midmorning and she was alone in the kitchen but for Anton who was brewing up a batch of leek-and-potato soup for the front takeout crowd.

The kitchen door swung open and she heard Karen's voice. She turned, surprised, for Karen didn't spend a lot of time in the kitchen being, as she'd admitted to Laurel, too much of a food junkie to trust herself.

"You'd be amazed how much food comes out of this kitchen in a busy week," she was saying in a tour guide tone. Laurel noticed the man at her side was nodding, looking around him with interest.

He was the most nondescript person she'd ever seen. Average height, average weight, average build, his hair so indeterminate a color you couldn't call it dark or light. On a woman it would be termed mousy, she supposed.

He wore the dullest gray suit she'd ever seen with a burgundy tie like the kind her dad wore. His face was pleasant without being in any way remarkable. He had no distinguishing marks. His glasses probably came from a big distributor. If someone had asked her to describe him, she couldn't have made him sound any different than half the male population.

"This is Laurel, our genius cake decorator. Laurel, Ron."

"Hello, Laurel." Even his voice was average, neither high or low-pitched, not loud or soft.

"You'd make a perfect spy," she said, not realizing she'd voiced the thought until she heard her own words.

Behind his glasses his gaze sharpened on hers and it was the first thing about him that was noticeable. He had beautiful gray eyes. But still, gray. "Pardon?"

She spent so much time with tiny plastic brides and grooms and animals made of fondant that she'd forgotten how to be around normal people. She felt the foolishness of her remark, saw that Karen was looking at her in a funny way, and blurted, "I read a lot of spy novels. I was thinking you'd be hard to describe. It's one of the things that makes a good spy." *Like keeping your mouth shut.*

Karen gave a social laugh, the kind that says, *let's move on,* but Ron seemed to consider her remark seriously. He said, "I'm a CPA. Being the kind of guy who disappears in a crowd is very useful for that profession, too."

"I'm sure it isn't. I mean, you're not…" Oh, Lord, what did she mean? A blush started to mount her cheeks.

"Laurel's very artistic," Karen said, in a way that suggested she wasn't good with words or people. Which was, of course, basically true.

"I can see that," Ron said, gazing at the cake behind

her. He was so incredibly neat, his not too long and not too short hair parted precisely, his shirt wrinkle-free, his shoes shining.

Today, as she often did, she wore clothes in Indian cotton that were already wrinkled, and she had a bad habit of getting icing in her hair. Her apron was certainly well-splotched with food coloring, bits of icing, and she noticed, glancing down at her plastic clogs, that there was a lump of marzipan on her toe. Next to this extraordinarily tidy man she felt like a disaster.

"This cake is incredible."

"Thanks. It's obviously a traditional cake, but I do all kinds."

"There's a book out front with samples of her work. You'll have to take a look when you get a second."

"I'd like that," he said.

"And this is Anton. He's one of Chelsea's people," Karen said, smoothly leading him to another part of the kitchen. They both admitted that Anton's soup smelled amazing, and then Karen whisked Ron away to meet the caterer who was upstairs.

Chelsea arrived in the kitchen herself not half an hour later and Anton said, "Why do we have a CPA prowling around the kitchen? We're not getting audited, are we?"

"No, of course not. Karen's dating him and I guess they got to talking and she decided to hire him."

"Karen's dating Ron?" Laurel gasped.

"Sure, why not?"

"I don't know, he seems so…" She couldn't find the word she was looking for. All she could come up with was "understated."

Chelsea grinned at her. "Well, they do say that opposites attract."

She thought of herself, One Big Mess—and a color-ful mess at that—and the tidiest, most understated man in the world and the strange, instantaneous attraction she'd felt toward him. "Yes, I guess you're right."

"SO, WHAT DID YOU THINK of our operation?" Karen asked Ron as they settled themselves back at her office. Lasagna was a treat she didn't allow herself very often, but she felt she needed to do something special for Ron after his embarrassment yesterday morning when Dexter had shown up at her door far too early in the day. Or maybe she felt some urge to punish herself by porking out on hundreds of calories of all her favorite things. So, she'd work extra hard at the gym tonight on her way home.

"You've got a great setup here. I think you're smart to have alliances with other businesses without setting yourself up as their employer. Makes your life a whole lot easier." He paused, took off his glasses and reaching into his pocket removed a cloth and began to polish the lenses. Then he replaced his glasses carefully. "Now, let's take a look at your accounting setup."

Karen was only too happy to have an outside expert look over her books and her systems. Ron was an easy person to have around, he didn't irritate her or ask her a million questions when she was busy, he simply got on with his work quietly.

And, much less quietly, she got on with hers.

"You want a live streamed video feed of your cer-emony to go online?" she said into the phone, roll-ing her eyes as she grabbed a pen. "Right, I'm sure it would be nice for the folks back home to watch you live. Mmm-hmm. Yes, I'm sure they do offer that in Las Vegas."

She sighed. Scribbled notes. It was always something. "It's not a service I get called on to do very often, but let me look into it and get back to you." And she hung up the phone.

"People want to have their wedding televised?" Ron asked, looking startled.

"It's like everybody wants their own reality show these days."

"Can you do it?"

She glanced up from her notes. "Provide a live feed? Oh, sure. I can do pretty much anything if it's legal and somebody's willing to pay for it."

"If I ever get married, I won't want it on TV."

Chelsea strolled in just then with a menu in her hands. "Won't want what on TV?"

"Ron doesn't want his wedding televised."

Chelsea blinked at him and then at Karen. "You're getting married?"

Ron looked understandably harried by this turn in the conversation and Karen had to laugh at his hunted expression. "No, we were talking about some of the outrageous requests I get from brides and grooms."

Chelsea stepped forward and placed the menu on Karen's desk. "This is the menu for the underwater crowd. Let me know what you think. I may have gone overboard on the fish courses." She stepped back and added, "I've always said if you call your business If You Can Dream It, you have to expect strange requests."

"There's a perfect wedding for everyone. I simply help make it happen." She looked up at Chelsea, so busy with her catering company that she wasn't getting her own wedding planned and decided this was the perfect moment to find out a few details subtly, so she asked Ron, "What would your perfect wedding be?"

He removed his glasses and polished them, which she was beginning to recognize as a stalling gesture. "Well, I can't say I've given it too much thought," he said to the lenses. "But now that my parents are both gone I suppose something very simple would suit me. A nice lunch, perhaps, for a very few friends and colleagues. And then my new wife and I would fly to Ireland."

"Ireland?" both women said at once.

He replaced his glasses and blinked at them. "Why not? I've always wanted to go there."

"Well, it's not exactly the top honeymoon destination." Chelsea smiled her lovely smile. "But maybe you'll find an Irish woman to marry."

"I only meant—"

"What about you, Chels?" Karen interrupted, knowing Ron was uncomfortable discussing something so theoretical. "What's your ideal wedding?"

"Honestly? I cater so many weddings and there's still so much post-divorce bitterness between my parents that my dream wedding is to hop on a plane, go to a first-class resort and be waited on." A dreamy expression floated across her face. "No sourcing fresh ingredients or worrying about food allergies. We'd laze around all day and order room service when we got hungry. Or just stay in bed all day. Perfect bliss."

"Why don't you do it, then?"

She fiddled with her engagement ring. "It's sort of complicated. First there was the whole fake engagement thing last year, and now that we're really getting married, David's entire firm is getting involved. Somebody's brother-in-law will play the fiddle, another has a friend who's a photographer, you know how it is."

"You wouldn't want to have your friends witness the event?" Ron asked.

"Not really. Weddings are starting to feel too much like work. We could always take pictures."

"Go to Las Vegas," Ron suggested. "You can have your own live TV wedding there."

"I'll keep that in mind." Then she turned the question to Karen. "Well? What's your perfect wedding?"

An image filled her mind. Her and Dex in a garden in June. The weather was perfect, the scent of roses hung in the air and she'd known in that moment that she was meant to be with the man beside her.

Apart from her mother refusing to sit anywhere near her father, and crying through the entire service, her wedding had been perfect.

"A garden wedding. But I already had my perfect wedding once. I doubt I'll get a second chance."

15

LAUREL WAS FEELING flustered when she arrived at work. With two wedding cakes to bake and decorate and a birthday cake for an obnoxious-sounding twelve-year-old boy who wanted a *Lord of the Rings* theme, she knew she couldn't waste any time. For a perfectionist, that was always difficult.

She changed her black boots for her plastic clogs, tied her hair back and slipped on a clean apron.

She was the first one in and the quiet kitchen, gleaming with stainless steel and hulking appliances still and quiet like sleeping giants, made her happy.

Her own small area wasn't completely uncluttered, however. A paperback novel sat in the middle of her counter. Puzzled, she picked it up. The book was well-thumbed, an old paperback that was clearly loved by its owner. She knew because she had a shelf of books like it at home.

The Thirty-Nine Steps, by John Buchan. The novel had a lurid red cover and when she opened it inside was a yellow Post-it note which said, "From a fellow spy novel enthusiast. This is one of my favorites. Ron."

If the man had sent her two dozen red roses she couldn't have been more thrilled. There was something so personal, intimate almost, about the sharing of one's own copy of an oft-read book. A tiny thrill went through her as she turned to the first page, imagining the times when Ron must have had his hands exactly here, turning the page for himself, perhaps in a coffee shop on a Saturday morning, or maybe sitting up in bed at night before settling to sleep.

Then the fatuous smile on her face snapped off like a light that's been switched off. What was she doing getting all romantic about this man? He was dating Karen. Chelsea had said so herself and Chelsea wasn't a person to make things up.

She closed the book carefully and slipped it into her bag to take home after work. She'd misread the situation. He was simply being nice. He wasn't showing interest in her.

He didn't want to date her, he wanted to be her book buddy.

With a sigh, Laurel hauled out a tub of cake flour and got to work creating yet another artistic fantasy that would be gobbled up in no time by greedy twelve-year-old mouths.

Hours later, she was well into the decorating when a soft male voice said, "That looks amazing."

She turned to find Ron looking over her shoulder. "Thanks. Do you know what it is?"

"The Eye of Sauron. From *Lord of the Rings*. I don't know how you did it, but the colors look like fire."

Like any artist, she was happy to have her work recognized. "Oh, good. I've got some really cool sparklers that will shoot red and orange sparks into the air. I figured a twelve-year-old boy is going to want something spectacular." She glanced up to find him still admiring the cake, and for a second she could imagine what Ron must have looked like as a twelve-year-old. "Thank you for the book."

"You're welcome. Have you read it?"

"No. I saw the movie once. During a Hitchcock phase I was going through."

He seemed pleased that she hadn't already read it. "It's a classic early spy thriller. You'll have to let me know what you think."

"I will." She continued piping red gel onto the rim of the eye.

"Maybe we could have coffee sometime?"

Her hand spasmed and splat: a great squirt of red spat out of her bag so the eye now had a huge red jujube of a tear hanging from it. "Oh, crap," she cried, grabbing a spatula and easing off the mess she'd made.

"I'm sorry. I didn't mean to startle you. Of course we don't have to have coffee. I thought you might like to discuss the book." He seemed as nervous and flustered as she felt.

She had no idea how to respond. She didn't even know what he was asking her. Was it for a date? Which is what she'd first assumed, but now she wondered if perhaps he hadn't meant anything more than a friendly coffee.

But what if she said yes, and it was a date, and then Karen might be upset and she loved her job here and didn't want to cause any trouble to a woman she liked enormously.

On the other hand, maybe it wasn't a date at all and she'd sound all stuck up and full of herself if she refused.

Which was why she pretty much stayed away from

the whole male/female personal interaction thing. It was all simply too confusing, like a game whose rules she'd never grasp.

She'd attempted to play chess a few times and felt absolutely bewildered. When was a playing piece allowed to go sideways and which ones could only go forward, she'd never quite understood. And as for that horse thing that went over and up, it was enough to drive a creative brain crazy.

Silence seemed to echo around the kitchen. It had never seemed so huge, or so empty. "Of course I'd like to discuss the book sometime," she finally managed to say, keeping her attention on the icing, but not daring to continue her task in case he said something that made her completely ruin her cake.

"You don't drink coffee?" he asked seeming a little puzzled.

"I love coffee," she snapped. One of them was being incredibly dense and she had a horrible feeling it was her.

"But you don't want to go out with me?" he finally asked with a kind of humble tone that made her glance up from the cake and meet his gaze.

"No. I would like to go out with you." She sighed. How could a woman spend so much time strengthening her core and believing in the essential oneness of all people and still be such a weenie? She decided to speak her truth. "But you're seeing Karen. At least that's what Chelsea said."

The second the words were out she regretted them. She didn't want Ron to think she'd been asking about him. How embarrassing.

He didn't make the obvious conclusion, but a puzzled frown settled on his face. "Karen's a wonderful person," he began. "But I don't think you could say we're seeing each other. Not romantically. We both realized that we'd rather work together than," he gestured helplessly, "you know."

"Oh."

"So, will you?"

The world made sense again. Speaking her truth was as wonderful as all the yogis in the world told her it was. "Go for coffee with you?"

"Yes."

"I hardly ever date," she admitted in a rush. "I'm not very good at it."

He breathed what seemed to her to be a sigh of relief. "Me neither. I am so happy we both like books. At least we'll have something to talk about."

She turned to him, not even realizing she still held the spatula. The connection she'd felt the first time she saw him was only strengthened by his words and she felt a rush of understanding. "I know exactly what you mean. Isn't that the worst part? Sitting there, racking your brain for something to say? And my mind always goes blank when I start to panic. I'll blurt out something ridiculous." He smiled at her and she suddenly recalled her brilliant conversational repartee of yesterday when she'd told a man she'd never met before that he could be a spy because he looked so innocuous. She supposed she didn't need to tell him another word about her little problem with blurting out the strangest things.

"Have you ever tried online dating?"

"No. I'd never have the courage." Her eyes widened in awe. "Have you?"

"Yes. I decided that mathematically it made sense to widen the scope of potential females as far as possible since I only meet a very narrow selection of women in my daily life."

"Impressive logic. How did it work?"

"Well, let's see, over the last four months I've gone on approximately twenty-five first dates."

"Twenty-five first dates?" Her eyes widened.

"Mmm-hmm. A few of them progressed to second dates, but nothing felt quite right."

"I don't know how you had the guts to keep going."

"I'm tenacious that way. Once I've determined on a course, I try to continue until I've achieved success or accepted that success is not possible. It's important not to give up too soon."

"Wow. Did you meet nice women?"

"Yes. Quite a few. It's how I met Karen."

She gestured wildly. "Get out of here. Karen went through with it? She tried online dating?" With a cry of horror she realized she'd swiped his neat blue and white striped tie with a slash of red icing gel. It looked like the tie had tried to slit its own throat.

They both looked down, but she was the one who gasped.

"Oh my gosh. I'm so sorry."

He continued as though the disaster had never taken place. "And through Karen, I met you."

He swiped his finger over the red gel on his tie and sucked the red goo off his finger. "I'd say it worked quite well."

"I've ruined your tie," she cried, holding her palms to her cheeks.

"Yes, you have. Let me know when you finish that book and we'll go for coffee." And he left looking surprisingly happy for a man wearing a suicidal tie.

16

When Karen waltzed into the kitchen, Laurel experienced a pang of uneasiness. She'd finished *The Thirty-Nine Steps* and was getting together with Ron Saturday morning for their promised coffee to talk about the book. But she only had his word for it that Karen and he were friends. She'd heard of men who used Internet dating to pull together their own personal harems.

Not that she could imagine Ron with a harem, but then how well did she know him?

Karen was in full business mode and checking timing on the various cakes that Laurel was making for her over the next two months. After they'd finished confirming delivery dates, she said, "Um, there's something I need to tell you."

Karen grabbed at her arm. "Oh, God. You look guilty. Please don't tell me you're leaving. I can't take it. Really. Your cakes are so spectacular, you're part of our success."

"No," she said, half laughing. "It's nothing to do with my cakes. I'm really happy here."

"Oh, that is such a relief." Karen slapped a hand

over her heart. Her manicure was perfect. Laurel really should think about getting one of those. She imagined her fingernails with that shiny pink finish, then couldn't. She wasn't the nail polish type. "I've finally got my dream team, I can't bear to lose one of you."

"It's more, um, personal." She looked down and suddenly wished she hadn't opened this conversation. She had no idea how to explain herself and felt foolish even trying.

"You can trust me," Karen said gently. "If you're in any kind of trouble…" The hand on her arm was both warm and soothing.

"Oh, I'm being stupid. It's nothing. Only Ron asked me out and then he said you and he… And I don't want to do anything you wouldn't feel comfortable with, because I am so happy here and…" Her voice petered out and she continued to stare at the floor until she couldn't stand it anymore and raised her gaze.

But Karen didn't look at all angry. More stunned. She said, "You and Ron?" the way a person might say "ice cream and horseradish?" As though the two things couldn't possibly belong together.

"You're surprised?"

"Well, yes, to be honest. You don't seem like you'd have a lot in common."

"We both like spy novels. And he has such nice eyes."

"Yes, he does." She tapped her pretty pink nails against her binder. "Wow."

Laurel couldn't gauge what "wow" meant. "So, are you okay with that?"

The wedding planner seemed miles away. She came back with a start. "Oh, absolutely. Ron and I met through a dating site but we had absolutely no spark. I think he's a very nice man and he's a talented accountant and I think we're becoming friends, but we're definitely not dating. I've hired him to do some work for us."

"Okay then, that's good."

"You and Ron. Who should know better than a wedding planner that opposites attract." She shook her head. "You'll have to tell me how your coffee date goes."

"How did you know we're having coffee?"

"That's how he always starts a relationship." Then as Laurel's eyes widened she hastily added, "At least, that's what he told me. It's not like I know him intimately or anything." She cleared her throat, obviously embarrassed. "Because, in case you're wondering, there was no, you know, between us."

Laurel was insensibly cheered by this news. Not that it was any of her business, obviously, if Ron and Karen, who had met before she'd ever met Ron, had hooked up. Still, she was glad they hadn't. She couldn't imagine how weird it would be to have sex with a man who'd also slept with a colleague who was the closest thing she had to a boss. Not that she was thinking of having sex with Ron. The very idea had her thinking as muddled as one of her crazy icing color experiments that failed.

LAUREL ALMOST MISSED the letter grade.

It wasn't until she'd made sure she hadn't left a bookmark or a smudge or anything that might lessen the book—or her—in Ron's eyes that she noticed the neatly penciled letter *A* marked on the inside back cover of the paperback.

An A and then a line of equally neat handwriting. It said: *Book that began a genre. Masterpiece?*

She loved the question mark at the end of *masterpiece,* as though he didn't want to give out superlatives too easily. Was the *A* a letter grade like a teacher would give a student paper?

She traced the comment with her fingertip. She thought of the way so many people throw out words like *masterpiece, genius, brilliant, groundbreaking* and so on and how rarely the rave was deserved. She'd often heard ridiculously over-the-top praise for her own efforts. But then, Laurel, who was modest about most things, knew that some of her cakes were, in fact, masterpieces. Which suggested that not only mastery of one's medium of work was necessary, but also something more. Some whiff of the creative, the unusual, that took a creation to a new level.

She'd never thought of herself in the same realm as artists—she made bakery goods to be consumed, her works of art were no more permanent than a sand castle or an ice sculpture.

And yet, she liked to think that she lifted the mere cake to a new level, infusing it with meaning and giving joy to those first viewing it and then consuming it.

A shy woman, she spoke through food.

Usually.

Sometimes other forms of communication were necessary and she never found it easy to converse. She was shy, loath from a child to put herself forward. She'd always admired bold women, like Karen, who could go out and meet new people, sell products and services, fight when she had to. Laurel was much happier alone in her corner of the kitchen putting her thoughts into icing rather than words.

Somehow, she recognized in Ron a kindred spirit. The fact that he'd made this short and measured judgment of a book appealed to her. She couldn't imagine him in a book club arguing the merits of chaining oneself to a stranger of the opposite sex as a way to solve crime, or discussing the sexual undertones of the book and how they related to the mores of the time. The very notion of Ron arguing in public about sexuality made her want to giggle.

And if he did want to discuss the book with her over coffee she knew she'd find herself tongue-tied and stupid.

But she had to say something. In the end, she took a Post-it note, so impermanent it wouldn't even leave a mark in the book, and below his A and comment she put her own. She said, after much thought and the wanton waste of half a dozen yellow sticky notes:

He's an ordinary man who, when forced to save his country, can do extraordinary things. As in so many thriller novels, things aren't what they seem to be on the surface. I think that's true of people, too.

She realized that her note was hardly significant literary criticism, but she didn't care. Her last line was more of a personal observation that had nothing to do with the novel but she was trying to tell Ron, in her own way, that she wasn't exactly what she appeared either. She hoped there was more to her than she could articulate.

As the date approached, she realized, she wanted to be different from all the other women he'd had a first date coffee with. Well, it stood to reason she would be because she was different from pretty much everyone she knew. But ever since Karen had told her that Ron started all his relationships with a coffee date, she'd decided that she wasn't going to tell her grandchildren that she and Grandpappy had got together over coffee in cardboard containers.

Nothing as permanent as love should start over anything involved in takeout.

Laurel wasn't a bold woman, but she was intuitive and if she'd learned anything in the years she'd studied and practiced yoga and meditation it was to honor her instincts. Of course, she could be wrong. Ron might be entirely wrong for her in the long term but she wasn't willing to ignore the strong feeling she had that the way they began would be important to their future.

Wanting to respect his idea of a first date, and yet still make it special, she called him.

When she picked up his business card to call him on Friday she accidentally left a purple icing thumbprint on the pristine card stock. When she identified herself he sounded instantly distressed. "You're not cancelling, are you?"

"No. I'm not. I have an idea. Instead of meeting at a coffee shop, I thought we might have a picnic."

There was a tiny pause. "A picnic coffee?"

"Yes. I will meet you at JFK Plaza." She didn't call it by its more familiar name, Love Park, named for the famous red-and-blue sculpture that spelled *LOVE* with the *O* tilted sideways.

"But it's almost winter."

"Wear something warm. I'll bring the coffee."

She was inordinately pleased with herself when he agreed. A first date at Love Park was the kind of outing to tell her grandchildren about. Even if the fountain wasn't operating, there was a great view of the city by looking northwest down the Benjamin Franklin Parkway, which was supposedly modeled after the Champs Elysées in Paris.

Laurel had no idea whether that was true or not. She'd never been to Paris, but she liked the idea that she could pretend. Besides, the art museum was at the other end of the plaza and she never tired of going there.

As she imagined their first date, thought about Ron, she began to create a perfect first cake to go with a perfect first date.

17

DEX HAD TAKEN TO texting her. She had no idea why, but the short, sexy, sometimes funny texts were getting to be a bad habit. Of course, it would be rude not to respond, so they began exchanging increasingly steamy messages.

Every time I see a takeout container I get hard, he texted.

She shut her phone and tried to ignore the surge of lust his words invoked. After her next appointment, she texted back: I can still feel your lips on my nipple.

The texts continued in this manner until she got one that puzzled her. Have dinner with me Friday night.

That's not sexy, she texted back.

Trust me, it will be.

She laughed aloud from the parking lot where she'd picked up the message. Replied, I don't trust you.

Hardly a minute had gone by when she had her reply. I know.

Even though a text message couldn't have a tone, she felt sadness coming from the words. As she looked at her phone, wondering how to reply, it rang.

"Hey," he said.

"Hey."

"So, dinner on Friday night is with the building owners and their wives. What do you say?"

"I'm not your wife anymore."

"I know. But you're a beautiful, interesting woman and I'd enjoy your company. Then, after dinner, we'll head to my hotel room and I'll demonstrate how much I've missed you."

I've missed you, too, she wanted to say. Instead she managed, "I think I can make it."

"Thanks. See you Friday."

SHE'D NEVER LOOKED MORE GORGEOUS, Dex thought as he escorted Karen into the restaurant. In her simple black dress, she somehow managed to appear both elegant and sexy at the same time.

He'd loved her sexiness when he'd first met her but he liked looking at her even more now she was a little older. He liked her confidence and the tiny lines at the edges of her eyes. They lured him in.

She was still a great corporate wife, too, he thought, watching her charm the building owners and make friends with their wives. What could have been a boring business dinner ended up being so much fun that everyone exchanged hugs at the end.

As they walked away making the short stroll to his hotel in overcoats and gloves, he said, "Thanks, that was more fun than I expected."

She squeezed his hand through their two gloves. "Thank you. Louise has a niece getting married next year. I schmoozed."

He laughed down at her. Her face was alive, her

cheeks pink with cold, her eyes sparkling. He couldn't help himself, he leaned over and kissed her full lips.

Her hand slipped up to his shoulder. "What was that for?"

"Schmoozing, smooching, I get confused."

"Come on, walk faster."

"You cold?"

"No. I want to get naked with you, and fast."

"That's my girl," he said, pulling her along the pavement at top speed. If he hadn't been staying on the seventeenth floor he'd have run for the stairs. As it was, the time spent waiting for the elevator was agony. Once the car came and they were inside and alone, he pulled her to him, kissing her hungrily, pulling off his gloves and slipping his hands inside her coat to feel her up.

She giggled, but slipped off her gloves to do some exploring of her own.

By the time they reached his room they were both panting. His hands were unsteady as they pulled off her coat, her dress.

When he saw her underwear he nearly expired. Under that classy dress she had the sexiest, barely-there black wisps of nothing that he'd ever seen.

He had them off in no time. She pulled back the covers and slid into bed, watching with frank enjoyment as he ripped his own clothes off and then rolled into bed. And paradise.

"Good thing we slept over at the hotel," Dex said next morning as they got ready to go down to the restaurant just off the lobby for a late breakfast.

"Why?" Karen asked.

"I don't have to worry about a certain CPA showing up this morning and forcing a showdown."

"Very amusing. To be honest with you, I think he dumped me for my cake decorator."

"Wow. She must be hot."

She swatted him and then gave him a shove that sent him sprawling. Luckily he'd had the forethought to grab her on the way down so they bounced onto the mattress together, still damp from the shower, still hungry for each other.

At some point, he knew they'd have to face up to what they were doing, but right now he was so happy to have her back in his life that he didn't want to go there. Having that sweet, willing body back in his bed was enough.

For now.

"Dex," she said, in a sexy, breathless tone, as she unbelted her robe.

He suspected breakfast would be late. And it would be room service.

18

WHEN RON ARRIVED for their coffee date, bundled in an overcoat, gloves and warm boots, his nose red from the cold, Laurel was already waiting on a bench. She got up and hugged him. He seemed a little taken aback but hugged her in return. She thought they fit nicely together, being of a similar height. When you were both average, average could be perfect.

She was wearing a man's winter coat that she'd picked up at a thrift store, a woolen hand-crocheted hat with a pink crocheted flower on the side that an aunt had sent her for Christmas, and purple mittens.

"This is a very nice spot," he said, seeming to see the LOVE sculpture for the first time in his life though he must have viewed it hundreds of times.

She was so happy he approved. He sat down on the bench and she reached into her bag and pulled out the thermos of coffee she'd made earlier. She only drank fair trade coffee, of course, and the brew was excellent.

She poured the coffee into china mugs she'd brought from home. They were pottery, made by hand at a women's collective in Guatemala and she loved their heft and the connection she felt with these women who were using their own artistic talents to make a better life.

She handed him his coffee, then realized she hadn't brought milk or sugar. "Um, I hope you like it black."

"I do."

Finally, feeling both bold and foolish, she unearthed a reusable cake box and handed it to him.

"What's this?"

"A little something to go with your coffee."

He opened it slowly and the grin that split his face made him look anything but unremarkable. He put down the coffee on the bench and removed his gloves so he could ease the cupcake out of the box.

She'd spent more time on that one cupcake than she'd spent on some four-tier wedding cakes. And his response was everything she could have hoped for.

The cake was spherical, with a flat spot on the bottom so it would stand. On it, she'd iced a simple variation of the continents, using blue gel with touches of green as the sea. On top of the world was a man made of fondant, a man with glasses and average-colored hair, in a gray suit—including a tiny blue-and-red striped tie— holding a briefcase in one hand and a gun in the other. She'd considered writing Top Secret on the briefcase but decided that was too obvious.

At first he simply looked at it, turning it every way so he could see the cake from all angles, not saying a word, but she could tell from his expression that he was pleased.

"This," he finally said, "is the nicest cake I've ever had. Thank you."

"You're welcome." She felt absurdly pleased. It was so rare for her to be present when her creations were consumed. Sometimes she never even met the final customers, she'd get commissions from Karen or Chelsea. To have the opportunity to watch someone she liked enjoy the fruit of her artistic vision and stove labor made her bubbly with excitement.

She anticipated his first bite. Would he be delighted at the cake she'd chosen for him? A plain white with lacings of hidden lemon flavor? She wanted to see him with icing smeared around his clean and proper mouth, to watch him gobble the tiny figure of himself she'd crafted so painstakingly.

After admiring the cake again, chuckling over the details and peering closer until his nose almost touched Africa, he said, "I can't believe how accurately you've delineated the continents in such a small space. It's quite remarkable."

Then, as carefully as he'd eased it out of the box, he began to replace the cake.

She couldn't stop herself from crying out in protest.

"What is it?" he asked, the thriller cupcake half in and half out of the box.

"You're not diabetic, are you?"

"I don't think so."

"Then why don't you eat it?"

He appeared as shocked at the idea of eating the cupcake as she was at the notion of him not eating it. "I can't do that, it's a work of art. I want to enjoy it. Make it last."

"You can't," she said, understanding the joy of her profession in that moment as she never had before. "Any more than you can make a perfect sunset last, or an amazing live concert, or a belly laugh. If you put that cake in the fridge until it rots, you'll have missed the joy of eating it. Please." She leaned over and touched his leg with her purple-mittened hand. "I made it for you."

He blinked at her slowly, then with a nod that contained a hint of sadness, he withdrew that perfect cupcake. And, after staring at it again from all angles, as though to commit the image to memory, he bit into Australia.

He didn't seem to mind that he got blue gel all around his mouth, didn't stop for a second to wipe up. Instead, he gave himself over to the pleasure of that first bite. "Mmm, mmm, that is so good," he finally said, licking his lips. "Usually commercial cakes are so disappointing, as though all the work went into the decorating for show, and then inside it's a boring cake. But this." He seemed unable to find words. Closed his eyes briefly. Then smiled at her. "I think I get it. You made an ordinary cake and filled it with a surprise flavor."

She nodded, pleased with his perception, and so he went on.

"It's like a thriller novel. Everything seems normal on the surface, but there are secrets to be uncovered. And the protagonist may seem like one thing on the outside but be full of surprises."

"Exactly. It's what I love about thrillers."

"And new relationships?"

He was gazing at her with those warm gray eyes that were anything but ordinary. Her stomach jumped and then settled. "Exactly."

He offered her the cake and she bit into the other side. Even she had to admit it was one of her tastiest, most inspired creations.

"This is a very different first date for me," he said, sipping from coffee that steamed in the cold air.

"I'm glad. How do they usually go?"

"I have a list of questions I can ask to keep the conversation flowing."

"Such as?"

"Tell me about yourself," he said.

"That's a good one to start with."

"I think so. Well? How about it? Tell me about yourself."

She sipped her coffee, thinking. What was there to tell, really, that a down-to-earth man like Ron would find interesting? When she reviewed her history, even with careful editing, she knew she'd sound like a flake. So she cut to the chase. "I'm a flake."

A quiet rumble that could have been a chuckle shook him. "Really? Have a bit of Antarctica."

He passed her the cake and she bit into it.

"I am, you know," she said around the flavor. "I don't like schedules or do normal things. I practice a lot of yoga—and I started a long time before it became popular, by the way. I've spent much of my life drifting."

She tipped back her head and contemplated the gray sky above. "All of it, really."

"Perhaps I could have some specifics?"

Suddenly, she laughed. "You see what I mean? I can't even have a normal conversation with details. I'm even a flake in conversation."

"I like that about you."

"You do?" If he'd told her he liked that her hair was four colors because she could never decide on one she couldn't have been more shocked.

"For the same reason I like your hair," he said, knocking her mouth wide open. As though he could hear her thoughts. "It's free and unfettered by rules and order. Oh, don't misunderstand me. I like order, I live by rules. Accountants have to, you know. Numbers don't have a great deal of room for whimsy. I saw you and something lightened in me. I think I have a tendency to be too serious."

She thought of the way he'd described his dating strategy to her, playing some kind of mathematical numbers game, and she had to agree.

"If you want whimsy, you've come to the right girl." She blew out a breath. Usually she was uncomfortable talking about herself, but she figured if she liked the guy enough to spend half a day making him a cupcake, she liked him enough to tell him about her life. So she tried.

"The only truly constant thing in my life has been cakes. I knew that's what I wanted to do when I was a teenager. But apart from that, I've moved around a lot, spent some time in India, never really been able to settle. My parents were hippies and somehow I never got out of the habit, I guess. I'm thirty-two years old and my longest ever relationship was two years. Everything I own fits into the world's tiniest apartment. Which I rent."

There was nothing left of the cupcake now but the little fondant man in the gray suit. Ron glanced at her as though he were about to ask if he could keep the little icing guy, but he surprised her, he leaned forward, holding the replica of himself between his thumb and forefinger. His eyes held hers. "I want you to take the first bite," he said softly.

Maybe it wasn't the sexiest remark a man had ever made to a woman, but it was the most erotic statement anyone had ever said to her. Perhaps because of the way he was looking at her. This buttoned-up accountant had sexual intent blazing in his eyes and she knew he was inviting her to do more than chomp a chunk of icing.

She leaned forward slowly. Opened her mouth. Like a perfect sunset, a great concert or a belly laugh, she knew this moment would be gone all too soon, and all she'd have would be the memory, so she tried to imprint every sensation. The feel of the cold breeze on her nose, the sound of traffic in the city, the cry of some hardy seabird in the distance, and the warmth of the man beside her. The expression of tender lust on his face, the way his lips curved slightly, a tiny smudge of blue lodged adorably on his chin.

He slipped her version of himself between her lips and she bit down, taking half of him into her, enjoying the burst of sweetness and the punch of almond. Because, as with the cake, she hadn't wanted the icing to taste predictable.

She licked her lips. He continued to gaze at her as he pushed the other half of his fondant self into his mouth and chewed. His eyes widened slightly as the unexpected flavor hit him, and they went squinty at the sides with humor.

Then he leaned over and, taking her chin in his hand, scanning her face for a long moment, he kissed her.

She was flighty and dreamy and whimsical and—deep to her core—romantic. She'd dreamed of Princes Valiant and Charming and every variation in between. The kind of men who rode steeds and crashed down doors and swept innocent, heart-pure maidens off their feet.

Ron wasn't anything like that. She couldn't imagine him on a steed. He seemed like the kind of guy who might be afraid of horses. She couldn't imagine him sweeping her off her feet, but he'd hold a door open for her, he'd be able to figure out even her income tax, which was a lot more practical in the real world.

It was only his kiss that made her feel like a fairy tale princess.

This was sweeping her off her feet, the way he took possession of her mouth, teased her with his tongue, so she tasted again the sweetness of sugar and almond, the hints of lemon from the cake.

She got the feeling he was as stunned as she was by the powerful attraction between them when their mouths met. She made a sound in the back of her throat, embarrassingly like the purr of a well-stroked kitten, and he pulled her in closer, until their bodies rubbed together. She felt all the frustration of winter. Coats and sweaters, possibly thermal underwear on one of them, which oddly enough didn't put her off but kind of excited her since it was so new and strange compared to what she'd been used to.

Guys who could unerringly find their Chi but didn't always have as much luck finding the clitoris.

Not that she knew a great deal about Ron, but somehow she felt he was the kind of man who, once shown, didn't forget important details like that.

His hands were rubbing up and down her back. She could tell he wanted to do more and was holding himself in check.

For her benefit or some odd notion of his own?

She rubbed her breasts provocatively against his chest, as provocatively as she could with all the layers between them and she was pretty sure he groaned in a quiet, self-contained way.

Hmm. She let her hand stray to his knee, slowly track north. He sucked in his breath when she brushed against a flatteringly hard erection. But he didn't pick up on her obvious invitation to do some more exploring of his own.

She thought about everything she knew about him and nuzzled a little closer. "How many dates do you usually have before you get intimate with a woman?" she asked softly.

For a second he didn't answer her. Then, with a trace of humor in his tone, he admitted, "Ten."

They kissed again. His glasses were fogging up as was her entire body.

"Would you ever make an exception to that rule?"

There wasn't a breath of hesitation. He panted, "Yes."

19

LAUREL AND RON STAYED on the bench necking for a while longer, until she couldn't stand it anymore, then she said, "I live in a tiny walk-up apartment."

"Does it have a bed?"

She giggled. "Yes."

"Let's go."

She thought he might have wanted to go to his place, but it seemed he didn't. So they went to her apartment in a Bohemian walk-up in the South Street area. They passed secondhand bookstores, places that sold nothing but incense, funky boutiques.

They entered the narrow hallway and walked up the three flights of stairs to her small apartment.

Ron walked in and hung his coat neatly on the brass hooks hanging on the wall. Then he helped her out of her coat and hung that, too. He neatly placed his gloves in the pocket of his coat while she dropped her mittens in the basket she kept for the purpose. When she pulled off her hat she felt her hair rise with static. She probably looked like a science experiment gone wrong.

"I like this place," he said, looking around. "It suits you."

"There's not much here," she said, trying to see it through someone else's eyes. Indian prints on the wall, her yoga mat stretched out on the floor. The modest shelf of books, mostly spiritual and thrillers. Only now, seeing it through his eyes did she see that it was an odd collection.

The ceilings sloped on both sides, so there really wasn't a lot of room to stand up unless you stayed in the center of the suite. Her bed took up most of one side of the apartment, covered in a tie-dyed spread she'd bought on impulse at a street market.

He glanced at the bed and away again. He wandered toward her books, studied the thrillers but didn't say anything. He stood there, staring at the books without uttering a word or even reaching for one, so that she wondered if he thought she had lousy taste in fiction.

"Would you like some tea?" she asked, seeing as now that they were away from that cold bench they didn't seem quite so hot for each other. Correction: *he* didn't seem so hot for her all of a sudden.

She didn't think it was because he didn't approve of her modest living conditions, so she had to consider other possibilities.

"Yes, I would like some tea," he said, as though they hadn't just filled up on coffee and cake.

She took the few steps to the tiny alcove where her kitchen consisted of a two-burner hotplate, a toaster oven and a microwave that she never used because she didn't believe that any appliance that cooked food that fast could possibly be healthy.

She plugged in the kettle and checked her stash of teas. "Happiness? Calm? Or peppermint?"

He looked at her. "You don't have one for Confidence?" he asked only half joking.

She turned to him. "Is that what this is about? Confidence?"

He shoved his hands in his pockets and turned his face up to the ceiling. "This is the reason I decided on a ten-date timeline."

"But—"

"You're so open, so giving. You live in the moment and I'm always planning for the future."

"I'm not sure I—"

"Laurel, I've only slept with two women." He shot the words out like bullets.

She forgot about the tea and moved toward him. "What difference does that make?"

The ceiling seemed to fascinate him, requiring all his focus. "And the last one was…a while ago."

He was so brave and honest, she felt warm all over and somehow protective of this sweet man who worked with numbers all day and read thrillers for excitement. She suspected he spent far too much time in his head. "Are you worried about—"

"I think I might be terrible in bed."

She resisted smiling. It would be counterproductive, she knew. If there was anything she'd learned to trust it was her intuition, and hers was telling her that a man who could kiss the way Ron did was not going to be a disaster in bed. But he was obviously feeling concerned. She'd messed with his careful plan, hadn't waited for ten dates to sleep with him, and she could see that he was feeling rocked out of his comfort zone.

So she contained her smile. She might be flaky and whimsical and a mess in a lot of real world ways, but there were a few things she knew to the core of her being. She rose on her tiptoes, linking her hands around his neck until he was forced to look at her, and kissed him softly. Instinctively, his arms came round her. "I'm very flexible, you know."

"Are you?" His voice was pitched higher than usual.

"Mmm-hmm. It's all the yoga."

His eyes lit with interest.

"When you're with me? It's impossible to be bad in bed."

And then she pulled his sweater over his head. And then his long-sleeved T-shirt, and finally his thermal underwear. She'd never been with a man who wore thermal underwear and for some reason she found it incredibly sexy.

His body was about what she'd expected. Pale skin. A nice compact body with the average amount of body hair, the average musculature. She'd always been a step outside of normal and it was nice to be with someone who was a step too far inside the rigid boundaries of the acceptable, the expected. The average.

He seemed completely happy to let her lead, so she dipped down to help him remove his jeans, his blue long johns, his thick socks.

She sighed with pleasure as she pushed him back onto her bed, leaving him in only his boxer shorts—boxers so dull they didn't even have funny sayings on them or hearts or something. They were plain navy cotton. The poor man needed her.

At least there was a nice tent in the middle of his boxers, so his supposed problems weren't anything that needed drugs most often advertised on the Internet.

He gazed at her with a kind of neediness and she realized he wanted to see her but was too shy to ask.

She probably should invest in something that would pass for lingerie, but she could no more see herself in silk nothings than she could imagine herself with a manicure. Her underwear was organic cotton, an oatmeal-colored camisole and simple matching panties.

But she did her best, stripping off her sweater slowly, putting some wiggle in it when she slipped out of her jeans, pulling off her socks and then climbing onto the bed beside him.

She was slim and slight, but she felt good in her body. It was toned and strong. Ron didn't say anything, but she thought he liked her body fine, too.

Leaning over, she kissed him until the guy who'd kissed her senseless on the bench was back.

He took his glasses off and reached to place them on her bedside table where they hit with a clatter in the quiet room.

Then she reached for the waistband of his shorts and peeled them slowly off him. And gasped.

He might be unremarkable everywhere else, but her Mr. Average CPA was definitely above average in some departments. What an incredible surprise.

She felt looser in her muscles than she ever had, more flexible, more…sexy. She peeled the cotton camisole over her head slowly, letting him watch his fill, which he did with his slightly myopic gaze fastened on her. She'd never felt so right with a man. His gaze on her was like a caress, heating her skin everywhere it alighted.

She slipped her panties down over her legs and snuggled into the bed beside Ron.

He turned his body toward her, touched her shoulder. "I never knew, under all those flowing things, you were hiding…that body."

Silent laughter shook her. The simple man or woman with much more to them than meets the eye; it seemed to her she and Ron were both like that.

"I could say the same."

She wrapped her arms around him, rubbing her naked body against his, enjoying the pleasure of her skin against his without any hurry. She loved foreplay, loved every second of it, so that when orgasm snuck up on her it was all part of a holistic experience.

Ron seemed a little shy, receiving her caresses but not initiating any of his own. "My hands and feet are cold," he warned her.

"Bad circulation, probably. I bet I can warm them up." And once she got him into yoga, which she fully intended to do, his circulation would definitely improve.

She took his hands in hers and found that they were a little cool, and placed them on her breasts. He tried to pull them back, telling her he didn't want her chilled but the minute her nipples hit his palms, he closed his hands over her breasts and began to knead the warm flesh.

His excitement was buzzing through his body, she could feel it. "I think I might…" he panted, but couldn't finish his sentence.

She thought he might, too, if he was worried about going off too soon, and since it was obviously a big deal for him she decided that the best course of action was to let him get rid of that first head of steam. She reached for her bedside table and the condoms she kept there, sheathed him efficiently without giving him a chance to protest.

Then she rolled on top of him and took him slowly into her body. His sheer size was an absolute joy to her, stretching and filling her. He made helpless noises indicating distress and she said, "I want you to come inside me, right away."

He lay below her staring up, all his half-uttered apologies stilled. "What did you say?"

"I really need to feel you come inside of me." She leaned down to kiss him full on the mouth. "Please. Now."

He groaned as though Santa Claus had just brought him the best gift ever, and grabbing her hips, thrust in and up, staying with her rhythm as she rode him.

It wasn't a long ride, she'd known it wouldn't be, and as he grew more frenzied in his movements she encouraged him. "Yes, I want you, now." When he exploded, she stayed with him through the roar of release and the tremors that shook him.

After they'd cleaned up, they lay side by side and he gazed at her ruefully. "I'm so sorry, I wanted to last longer but—"

She kissed him.

"Feel better now?"

"Immeasurably."

He rolled over and kissed her, and, as she'd hoped and half expected, his cock was already rising for more action.

"Do you have to be somewhere?"

"Not for hours," he said.

"Then quit apologizing."

He chuckled, running his hands through her crazy hair. "Why don't I make love to you instead?"

She loved his intelligence. "That would be a much better use of your time."

As she'd already suspected, he knew exactly where the clitoris was and it seemed to fascinate him. She found that he was particularly good at focusing on her needs and pleasures.

Maybe he was a little rusty at first, but he soon grew comfortable and there was definitely chemistry between them. She'd probably been with technically superior lovers in her time, but she'd never had more fun in bed.

Never.

He was indeed a thriller.

RON DIDN'T LEAVE until the next morning. "Well?" she asked as she watched him get dressed. "How do you think our first date went?" She felt sleepy and satisfied, her entire body replete. She supposed a man who worked with accounts and spreadsheets all day had to be good at focusing and staying on task and she'd found that once he got over that first eager climax he'd been as focused and generous as she could have wished.

"I think," he said, as though giving the matter profound thought, "that was the best first date of my life." He regarded her for a moment, his eyes twinkling behind his glasses. "If I were a man given to hyperbole, which I am not, I might characterize that as the greatest first date in all of history."

She hadn't thought he could make her feel giddy, but she was wrong. A foolish grin split her face. "Really?"

"Really."

"Me, too."

"Oh, I almost forgot," he said and went to his jacket. From the right pocket he withdrew an early John le Carré novel. "Have you read this?"

"No," she lied because she wanted to get her hands on his copy. When he handed her the book, the first thing she did was flip to the inside back cover and find the letter grade and accompanying comment. A again. How they made her smile, his comments. So measured, so restrained.

"Do you grade all your books?"

"Yes. It's a habit of mine."

"Do you give every book an A?"

"Of course not. I only keep the books I consider a B or above."

"So you're sharing with me your favorites?"

"Yes." Maybe some men wooed a woman with roses and candlelight dinners, but for her, this was so much better. He was sharing the books he loved, letting her put her hands where he'd put his. Even sharing his comments about the book, which she instinctively knew he wouldn't do easily.

"Do you ever give a book an A+?"

"Not so far. My feeling is that if you give an A+ and then a better book comes along, the A+ loses its meaning. I'm not of the opinion that one can keep adding pluses. So the A+ is the greatest spy novel I've ever read."

"And it's still out there?" For some reason she found the idea charming. And optimistic.

"I suppose, if it exists, that it's still out there, yes."

"Or hasn't been written yet."

"Another possibility."

"How do you decide to give a book an A?"

He was on safer ground here, she could tell.

"I have a grading scale. A book has to answer all the questions it sets out, if it's a mystery, the reader must have had the clues to solve the puzzle. The writing must be of high quality, obviously, and the general story must interest me. That's a subjective way to rate a book, but it's the one I use."

She got out of bed, naked, but she didn't care and walked over to him.

She put her arms around him and thought she could never have enough of this man. She barely knew him and yet she knew him so well.

"I had such a great time," she said.

He pulled back slightly so he could see her face. "You are the A+ I never thought I'd find."

20

"No, NO, NO!" Karen yelled at her computer screen.

"What is it?" Dee cried, running in at top speed to where Karen was yelling obscenities at an electronic device, no doubt looking as demented as she felt. "Has your system crashed?"

"Yes!"

"I'll call the tech guy. Don't worry, I'm sure they can restore your hard drive. And remember, we got that automatic backup after the last time."

"Not that system." Karen waved her away. "It's personal, not business."

Dee blinked at her for a moment, then seemed to appreciate she was having a really bad day and backed away. "Ah. Well, if you need me, I'm out front."

"Thanks. Sorry for the panic." She had to get a grip. She really, really had to get a grip.

System crash. Dee had the terminology right, but it was her internal system that was crashing. The one that kept her functioning and sensible. All it took was one text message.

From Dexter. He'd called earlier to say he was back

and staying the weekend. Since she hadn't seen him for over a week, she was more pleased than she should be to know she'd be seeing him tonight. She was just beginning to think that this sex with Dex the sexy ex was actually working out when he had to go and ruin everything.

Again.

The text was still on her phone. She called it up and stared at it again. Do you want to spend Christmas together?

Why did he do this to her? No, why did he still have the power to do this, to make her feel young and foolish and in love again? Did he have any idea how very badly she wanted him? How desperately she'd tried not to notice when he wasn't in town and she wasn't seeing him.

But Christmas? That was what married people did. She knew exactly what it would be. A big dinner with family who would all ask impertinent questions, and then he'd suggest a quick trip. Skiing for a few days, or the Caribbean. They'd spend New Year's Eve shushing atop a mountain, or sailing under a heavy, golden sun. It sounded heavenly.

She couldn't do it. She could not go down this path again.

As much as she'd tried to deny it, she had to admit to herself that she wasn't simply enjoying casual booty calls with her ex. She was making love with the man she loved with all her heart.

And that heart couldn't take another break.

She decided that Dexter Crane had been put on this earth to drive her insane.

And that it was her job to cut him off at the pass.

She didn't text back.

But as the hours crawled along she could think of nothing else but getting naked with the man who'd given her so much physical pleasure and so much emotional pain.

When she booked a wedding night suite for a soon-to-be married couple, she ended up drifting into a reverie where she recalled her own wedding night. In fact, she didn't think they'd stopped making love for three days, practically pausing only to eat and shower.

Well, she wasn't going to go running over to his hotel tonight. She'd moved on. She was a woman in her prime who wasn't getting regular sex. That was the only reason Dex's call had her squirming on her office chair all day imagining all the things he could do to her at night. All she had to do was go to him.

Which she had no intention of doing.

What she needed was a distraction.

She'd be so busy tonight that she wouldn't have time to think about Dex waiting for her in his hotel room. All hot and naked and… No. She wasn't going there.

Around four, Karen stomped into Chelsea's office feeling twitchy and irritable.

Since Dexter had stormed back into her life and, even worse, into her bed, she'd been feeling this way a lot. "What's up?" Chelsea asked in surprise when Karen let out a frustrated howl as she entered her friend's private space.

"We're going partying tonight."

"We are?"

It was a Friday, and a perfectly reasonable request, except that she and Chelsea had never partied together before. "Remember when you promised me a girls' night out?"

Chelsea slapped a hand over her mouth. "Oh, my gosh, I did. I forgot."

"Well, we're going to have it tonight."

"We are?" she repeated.

"Yes. We are."

Chelsea had appeared mildly surprised, but now a frown of concern pulled her perfectly maintained eyebrows together. "Honey, what is it?"

"He wants to spend Christmas with me. I could kill him."

"That jerk." But she seemed a little amused and her words didn't hold much heat.

"It's not funny. I thought we were having a fling, no strings, no commitment, simply sex when we're both around and feel like it. Now he wants me to spend the holidays with him. But it's impossible."

"Why?"

The truth burst from her. "Because I still love him."

"I know," Chelsea said, her brown eyes warm with sympathy. "I know." She put a hand on Karen's and said, "Do you think maybe he loves you, too? Why else would he ask you to spend the holidays with him? Honey, he wants you back."

"But he cheated on me."

There was a pause. "I don't know what's right for you. But don't you think that sometimes, people can change?"

Shock held her speechless. "Are you suggesting I should take the cheating liar back?"

"I think, maybe, he's trying to get your forgiveness, maybe a second chance. Of course, it's up to you to give him one."

"Men don't change," she said, thinking of her father and the destructive pattern of his relationships.

"Sure they do. People change all the time. Sometimes, for the better."

"I'm so mixed up. I can't see him right now."

"And you don't have to."

"Maybe if we go out tonight, I'll have the strength to stay away from him."

"Well, I did promise you a girls' night out."

"Good. Besides, it's time we took control of our lives. You, with a guy who won't commit, me, even poor Laurel, what are we? Some kind of wimps? We sit around and wait for men to decide our futures?"

"Did I hear my name?" Laurel floated in all wispy and fragile, with a streak of purple icing in her hair that looked as though a psychotic hairdresser might have put it there.

"Yes. You're coming too," she decided on the spot. "I was telling Chelsea that we need a girls' night out. The three of us. All we ever do is work and where's it getting us? I'm sleeping with my ex-husband—"

Laurel's eyes widened in shock. "You are?"

"Yes. But you can't tell anyone that because it's insane."

"Who is—"

"Never mind." She waved an imperious hand. "The point is, it's got to stop. And look at you two." She waved a slightly shaky hand between the two of them. "Chelsea's the most beautiful woman I've ever seen and she's engaged to a guy with commitment problems—"

"Actually," Chelsea began, but Karen cut her off.

"And you?" She turned to Laurel. "You're like Cinderella, Sleeping Beauty, Rapunzel, all those fairy tale princesses you put on cakes. All your passion is going into butter cream!"

She hauled in a breath. "This has to stop."

Laurel took a step backward. "I'm sort of see-ing—"

Karen interrupted as though she hadn't spoken. "That is why, we three are going out tonight and we will have so much fun that men will be a distant memory."

Laurel and Chelsea glanced at each other and if she wasn't so mad she couldn't see straight she'd probably have been able to interpret their expressions. As it was, she didn't really care what they were thinking. Her plan was a good one. "This is exactly the thing we need to get us all unstuck."

Chelsea frowned. "You know, I have an idea. How about the three of us head back to my town house for a bottle of wine." She glanced at Karen. "Or two."

"Sitting around drinking wine in the town house you share with the man who won't commit to marrying you isn't my idea of a fun time." She shook her head. "I'm going downtown. Who's with me?"

For a long moment no one said anything. Finally, Chelsea closed her computer file with a click. The light caught the big honking engagement ring on her finger that had sat for too long waiting for its mate, rather like its owner.

"I'm with you. You're right, it will be fun."

"I don't really…I'm not sure I can…" Laurel began then, taking a deep breath, she said, "I'm in."

Chelsea said, "Thanks, Laurel," which seemed like a stupid remark, but Karen was too happy to know they'd seen the light to cause an argument.

"Good, that's settled then."

21

THE TECHNO MUSIC in the club beat into Karen's body with the thrusting insistence of her mood. Her blood picked it up, her hips joined in, already swaying.

"Oh, boy," Chelsea said behind her.

After enjoying a couple of cocktails in an after-work hangout, she'd suddenly remembered she wanted to check out this club as a possible wedding venue and dragged the women along.

The place was dimly lit, and crowded with a restless, moving throng of people, mostly in their twenties and thirties with a smattering of older people and teens with fake IDs.

The dance floor was a pumping, swaying crowd. It was a good size, the wedding planner in her noted. A waft of air-conditioning brushed the exposed skin above her low-cut top, reminding her how hot her skin felt everywhere.

She would not think of Dex touching her there, of Dex, even now, waiting for her in a hotel only blocks away from here. She would not.

"I think there's an empty table in that corner over

there," Laurel said, gesturing into the quiet area at the back.

"We'll sit at the bar," Karen decreed and without waiting for argument she led the way into the most crowded part of the club apart from the dance floor.

When they got to the bar, she ordered a Kamikaze. She wasn't entirely sure what was in the cocktail, but the name sounded full of alcohol, and deadly, which was good.

Chelsea ordered a Pernod, and Laurel, after dithering through the menu, and Karen thinking that if she ordered herbal tea or something she'd have to smack her, settled on a glass of white wine.

"This is fun," she shouted over the music. "Isn't it?"

"Really great," Chelsea said, sounding absentminded. Karen saw that her hands were beneath the level of the bar and immediately made a grab for them, yanking away Chelsea's cell phone before the other woman could stop her.

"No texting," she ordered.

"I was telling David that I won't be home until later. That's all."

"Huh. I've got a few things to say to David myself."

Laurel seemed as though she'd gone to bed in a normal universe and woken up on a different planet where she didn't know the rules. "You're acting a little strange," she finally said in her soft, tentative way.

When Chelsea turned to talk to her in a low voice, no doubt about how Karen was having some kind of breakdown, which she had to consider was a possibility, Karen took the opportunity to finish Chelsea's text and push Send. Overhearing the last of her companions' conversation, which contained the words *complicated* and *confused* she said, "It's not complicated. And I'm not confused."

"Do you want to dance?" a thirty-something guy asked her.

"Yes," she told him. "I would." Then she turned to her companions. "Isn't this better than the Internet?"

Karen loved dancing, she'd forgotten how much.

She was soon joined by her friends. Chelsea danced in a more restrained manner, but you could see that she was comfortable with her body and enjoyed moving in it. Laurel seemed to hear a different song than they did, something softer and more melodic. She floated through the rhythm rather than conforming to it.

Her partner moved over to dance with Chelsea and then a blond boy, for boy was all he was, stared at Karen, dancing his way closer until he said, "You know who you look like?"

"Your mother?"

But he hadn't heard her. "Amy Adams." He considered her for another moment. "With bigger breasts." And he moved closer, dancing as near her as he dared.

"Whose idea was this?" she shouted to Chelsea who drilled her pointer fingers her way in time to the beat.

He was adorable, though, with big blue eyes and a flop of hair. Skin so smooth she doubted he had to shave every day. Still, he was dancing with her and he was cute.

"How old are you?" she asked him.

"Twenty-five." He said it so fast she knew it was a lie.

"I'm too old for you."

"I've been with an older woman before," he said with immense pride.

"Yeah? How old was she? Twenty-six?"

He grinned at her. "You're so sexy. I am really into you right now."

"You are balm to my ego. But I think that girl over there is trying to get your attention."

He glanced behind him at a pretty brunette who was gesturing to him.

"Oh, yeah. Don't move. I'll be back." And he was gone.

He was replaced by a second, older version of himself. This guy was probably thirty. And shaved every day.

"I was watching the way you move," he said as he came up to her as though he had every right to invade her personal space. "You're a very sexy woman."

"So I hear."

"I'm serious. You radiate sex. It's really powerful. I want to take you home and do you, right now." He grabbed her hand and twirled her. She kind of liked the macho way he assumed control of her.

"I'm John."

"Hi, John."

"I'm only in town for a couple of days. What do you say?" There wasn't a lot of finesse in the way he eyed her the way the big bad wolf eyed Little Red Riding Hood but it was nice to know she had options if she wanted nothing but sex.

The gleam in his eye was purely carnivorous and on some deep level she responded. It was nice to be reminded that she was still a desirable woman. She spent so much time obsessing about what was wrong with her and wishing she was taller and thinner that she forgot she'd always drawn male attention.

Keeping a man's attention for a lifetime seemed to be the problem.

She glanced around. Chelsea was making nice to an older man who had "freshly divorced" written all over him, and Laurel was now dancing with the fresh-faced blond kid.

She was suddenly filled with affection for both these women who were here for her, since it was clear neither of them would have chosen to come out dancing if she hadn't made them.

Her partner nuzzled her neck, which she found mildly annoying. Where was the teasing, the finesse, the… Oh, she had to stop thinking about Dex.

"What's your name again?" she asked.

"John." He laughed down at her. "And you have a great ass. You know that, right?"

"Right now, I don't know anything."

He seemed to take that as a come-on rather than what it was: a true expression of how she was feeling, a wail of despair from some deep unexplored part of herself.

"I've got a bottle of scotch in my room. It's open so I can't take it on the plane. Might as well drink it. Come on up."

"Wow," she said. "It's a tempting offer, but I don't think so."

"Why not?"

"I can't leave my friends. But thanks." She pulled away. "Have a nice evening."

"No. Wait. You're so hot. I could make you feel real good. Let me tell you what I'm going to do to you." He tried to kiss her, but she resisted.

"Some other time."

Laurel and Chelsea were as ready to leave as she

was, so they jumped in a cab and headed out into the night.

"You know, that was fun," Chelsea said. "We should hang out more."

"It was fun. Thanks for coming out with me. I needed the company."

"Why don't you stay at our place tonight? There's a very nice guest room. You'd be welcome."

"No, thanks. I'm not good company right now. I think I'll just go home to bed or something."

The cab drew up outside the town house Chelsea shared with her fiancé, David. She opened the door and as she exited leaned in to give Karen a hug. "Be careful about that 'or something.'"

She dropped Laurel off next, and then the cab driver asked, "Where to?"

She opened her mouth to give him her home address. She was certain that's what she intended, but what came out of her mouth was the name of the downtown hotel where Dex was staying.

22

DEX DREAMED he was on a construction site and the crew was really going at it with the hammers. It took him a minute to realize he'd been wakened by pounding. He glanced at the bedside clock and wondered who had visitors at two in the morning?

Another minute went by before he realized it was his door taking the pounding.

No doubt some partiers had the wrong room. He yawned and rolled out of bed, somehow knowing from the intensity of the banging that ignoring whoever was on the other side of his door wasn't an option.

He dragged on the hotel robe and padded barefoot to the door. An eye to the peephole showed him, not partiers, but Karen, dressed to kill.

Even through the distorted lens of the peephole he felt her sensuality. A woman only came banging on a man's door at 2:00 a.m. for one reason. He was hard before he had the door opened.

She didn't tumble in his arms as he'd half expected, or open a coat to show she was naked underneath, a persistent fantasy that she'd never yet fulfilled. She pushed past him like a dynamo, he could feel her body heat as she brushed past him and a scent that smelled like sex and danger.

"I didn't think you were coming," he said on a yawn. He didn't bother to tell her that he'd waited like a fool for her to show up until all the ice in the bucket cooling the champagne had melted. He'd finally called down to room service for a burger and a beer and watched a Flyers game on TV.

"I wasn't," she said. "I went out with the girls, but this guy came on to me on the dance floor. And his body was the wrong shape and his smell was all wrong. And all I could think about was that I wanted you." There was something about the way she wailed that last line that told him everything he needed to know. The woman he loved, loved him right back.

Then she did tumble into his arms. Or maybe he pulled her in, it was impossible to tell.

All he knew was that she was a bundle of heat and needs and passion and when his mouth closed over hers it felt right. She tasted right. She smelled right. The thought of her being with anyone else made him crazy, but he was also honest enough to admit to himself that the idea of her being out there, attracting the attention of other men, and then rejecting them to come here to him was darkly exciting.

He pushed his hands down the front of her top and released her breasts, taking them into his mouth, sucking and licking her the way she liked, easing her closer to the bed. But she didn't want to be eased anywhere.

She reached into his robe and took him into her hand. Her skin was so hot when she closed over him. Then, her eyes sparkling with excitement, she pushed the robe off his shoulders so it fell to the floor and then knelt before him and took him into her mouth.

Oh, if he'd thought her skin was hot it had nothing on her mouth. He wondered if any two people had ever known each other as intimately, had fit together so perfectly, knew so instinctively what the other craved.

She loved him with her mouth, teased him with her tongue, and he let her control him until he was mindless. But being taken by this woman in her crazy mood wasn't good enough.

In some primal part of himself he recognized the need to give as good as he got. Hauling her to her feet, he pushed her backward, angling her so her butt sat on the arm of the maroon-and-blue striped armchair. He stripped off her panties in one practiced motion. He started to lean in, to use his mouth on her as she'd used hers on him, but what he saw in her eyes stopped him.

Slowly, he leaned forward and kissed her. He didn't say the words, not yet. Instead he took her by the hand and led her to the king-size bed. He made love to her as he never had before. Letting his emotions out, through his skin, his mouth, his hands. They were both trembling when they came together.

A slow grin spread over her face. "Whatever you did, do it again."

He smiled at her tenderly. "You never replied to my text. Spend the holidays with me."

"Why would I do that?"

"So we could spend some time together. We could take off and go skiing or spend a few days in the Caribbean. I'd rub suntan lotion on your body and—"

"We're not a couple anymore, Dex."

"Are you sure? I still love you."

She turned her face away from him. "No."

"I never stopped. And when you accused me of cheating I was so angry and so hurt I never fought hard enough for you. For us. Karen, I want another chance."

"I can't deal with this right now," she said, jumping out of bed and grabbing her clothes, pushing them on at random.

"Here's the thing," he said as she pushed her feet into her heels and simultaneously stuffed one arm into her coat sleeve while opening the door with the other hand. "I think you love me, too."

"I—I wish you'd never come back, Dex."

"If you leave me again, I won't come chasing you. Kiki, don't do this."

His answer was the door shutting behind her.

CHELSEA LET HERSELF INTO the town house. The muted buzz of a TV told her where to find David. After watching her friend lose the program today she really needed the calm good sense of the man she loved.

One thing about David, he never went on any psychological roller-coaster rides.

She walked in to find him with a beer in his hand watching the replayed highlights of a Flyers game. She went over and put her arms around his neck. "How you doing?"

"Just sitting here being an emotional cripple. Yourself?"

She eased to sitting beside him on the tasteful couch his designer had picked out before she met him and that she'd made more personal with pillows and a colorful throw.

"Did you have a bad day?"

"No." He glanced at her, looking sort of huffy. "It was fine until around ten tonight."

"What happened at ten?"

"You sent me a text. Remember?"

"Yeah, I sent you a text saying I'd be home late." A horrible feeling gripped her. "Karen wanted to go out with the girls and she's my friend. I went. We didn't have plans or something, did we?" She wasn't one to forget social engagements and besides, they usually checked in with each other during the day. He hadn't mentioned anything when they'd spoken earlier.

"I figured I'd wait until you got home to see if you were drunk or something."

"I had two Pernods. I am not drunk. What is going on?"

"You seriously don't remember?"

"Remember what?"

He pulled out his cell phone and showed her. There was her text. Which she remembered writing. It said, I'll be home late. Eat whatever's in the fridge. That part she remembered perfectly well. Then the message continued. And why don't you man up? Get married like you promised instead of avoiding the issue like a typical male emotional cripple.

She put the phone down on the table. "Ah," she said.

"I don't understand. You know I want to get married. I've tried to set a date about twelve times but you always have an excuse. Everybody at work is starting to piss me off with their offers to help and somebody's cousin who's a photographer and have we decided on the color of ribbon for the freaking pew bows and I don't even know what pew bows are."

"I know, but you see—"

"I wasn't ready last year, and I know how stupid it was of me to pretend to get engaged to you so that I could get a promotion at work. How many times do I have to apologize?"

"You don't have to—"

But there was no point trying to interrupt him. He was on a roll and she got the feeling this was a rant he needed to get out of his system.

"I was blind and so incredibly focused on my career that I forgot what life was about. Then I met you and I was so busy trying not to get married to you that I didn't notice I was falling in love with you and that all I wanted in the world was to be with you forever."

"Oh, David." She felt love and tenderness for this man well inside her.

"But ever since we got engaged for real you've been avoiding the issue of getting married. And now, now that I've practically given up asking you when it would be convenient to marry me, you send me a text like that?" He shook his head, "Just tell me. What do I have to do to make you my wife?"

She stared up at him and thought that the great thing about loving someone was that they could always surprise you, no matter how well you figured you knew them.

"I hurt your feelings."

"You're damn right you hurt my feelings. Who wants to be called an emotional cripple?"

"No. I didn't." She picked up the remote and muted the TV. "I didn't write that part of the text. Karen took my phone away from me. I didn't send you that message. If you'd read it over a second time you'd probably have realized that."

He blinked at her. "Karen wrote it?"

"Yes."

"Karen? The wedding planner?"

"That Karen."

"But— I thought she liked me."

"She does like you. She's going through something with her ex-husband and she was in a crazy mood, not helped by mainlining a couple of drinks called Kamikazes."

He sat down. Still not as close to her as she'd like, but at least they were on the same couch. "So, you didn't write that text."

"No. I don't think you're an emotional cripple." She couldn't resist teasing him a little. "Because I fixed you. You totally used to be an emotional cripple. Now you're not." She leaned over and put her hand over his. "I didn't realize getting married was a big deal to you. I'm sorry."

"Well, it's…a man has certain expectations. If he asks a woman to marry him and she accepts…" He drilled her with his eyes. "I mean for real and not in some bogus fake fiancé way—"

"Right."

"Then he expects that she'll find a weekend in her busy schedule to marry him." He leaned forward, so earnest and eager that her heart went squirmy. "You know, you have to book these places six months in advance and then there's the photographer to book and well, the pew bows."

"I know. I've been putting everything off. I have."

His hands tightened painfully on hers. "Tell me the truth. Are you having second thoughts?"

Her heart began to hammer. "No." She couldn't bear it if he did so she asked very quickly. "Are you?"

"No. I love you. I don't want to wait another half a year to be married to you."

"Are you really stuck on a big wedding?"

"For all I care we could go down to the courthouse and get married on our lunch hour."

"Really?"

"Yeah. Of course. Weddings are for brides." He seemed to consider that statement. "And families."

"And friends." She flopped back on the couch still holding his hands. "I keep thinking I'm too busy to get married but the truth is I am avoiding it. Weddings are starting to become associated with hard work in my mind."

"But I need to seal the deal."

"Seal the deal? What am I? An insurance policy?" As the top salesman for an insurance firm, he had a bad habit of thinking in sales speak.

"Okay, okay. I want to marry you."

She glanced up at David under her lashes thinking that marriage to him was never going to be dull. He had that look in his eye, the one that suggested they'd be naked and she'd be seeing stars before too long. He only had to look at her like that to get her hot. "I might have to try you out first."

David made a sound deep in his throat, part moan, part growl. "You are the sexiest woman on seven continents." He took a fingertip and traced the line of her V-neck silky top that revealed just a hint of cleavage. He trailed the line of her shirt down to where it ended and then nudged the fabric a little farther.

"Yeah?" She felt liquid and sexy and his eyes were getting that heavy-lidded expression that made her melt. She traced her hand up his thigh. "I remember when you tried to pick me up on the street."

"Greatest night of my life," he said.

He picked up the remote, and pushed another button. Music flooded the room. He pulled her gently to her feet and pulled her against him. She closed her eyes and settled her head against his chest, moving with him. He simply led her around the floor, her body pressed to his. He took a lock of hair that had fallen across her cheek and wound it around his index finger. He traced her lips. "You're the sexiest, most beautiful woman I've ever seen." It sounded like he was telling her the truth in his heart.

"Oh, David," she said, and lifted her face for his kiss.

And as he wrapped his arms around her, she realized she was tired of playing games. So she'd have a complicated wedding with parents who hadn't been able to put their bitter divorce behind them, interfering but well-meaning work colleagues and David's parents whom she loved, but who didn't have enough to do now they'd retired. They wanted this marriage so badly they'd offered to pay for it, organize it and host it. She'd found her future mother-in-law knitting yellow baby booties and when she'd claimed they were for a friend, she hadn't quite believed her.

But really, in the big scheme of things, was she going to let all those things stop her from marrying the man she loved?

"Are you sure you can put up with me forever?" she asked him, her head still against his chest where she could hear his heart beating its steady, reliable rhythm.

"Yes. I want to be with you forever. Longer if I can

figure out how that part works." He pulled away long enough to look down into her face. "I love you."

"Let's get married," she said.

23

KAREN CREPT into the kitchen as though she were about to commit a felony. Laurel watched in surprise as she crossed to her side, checking over her shoulder before speaking.

"Where's Chelsea?"

"She said something about driving out to Kennett Square. She went to source mushrooms."

"She drives miles out of town for mushrooms." Karen shook her head. "And I think I'm obsessed with food."

"Did you need her for something? She's got her cell phone with her."

"No. I'm having lunch with her fiancé and I don't want her to know anything about it."

Laurel blinked, pausing from airbrushing clouds onto a sky-blue background to concentrate her full attention. Since Friday when they'd had their girls' night out, Karen had been acting strange. Now she was becoming seriously worried. "You're dating Chelsea's fiancé?"

Karen's laugh was sudden and loud. "No, not that

kind of a date. As if he'd ever look twice at me when he's got Chelsea."

"It's weird they don't get married."

"It's men. They can't commit. They're all like 'too many first dates, Ron.'" She suddenly stopped, looking at Laurel fully for the first time. "Oh, that was rude. I forgot you were one of them. Um, how did your coffee date go?"

Laurel wondered if it was even possible to put into words how that first coffee date had gone, decided it couldn't be done, not without a thesaurus and a lot of time. Besides, their relationship was all so new and special she didn't want to spoil it by talking too soon. She settled on "Fine."

"Really? I wouldn't have thought you two would have much in common. But that's great. Are you seeing him again?"

Laurel was an honest person, but she didn't feel any need to share with Karen that apart from when they were working, she and Ron spent most of their time together. When they'd exhausted themselves making love, sometimes they read together in bed. He'd even taken her to the house he'd inherited from his parents, introduced her to his dog, Beth, and she was helping him make the family home over into his.

After her telling him his ideas were too conservative and him telling her that hers were too wild, they were meeting there tonight with a designer. She was flattered that he wanted her input, but she thought they both knew she'd end up living there one of these days.

Not that he'd said anything, or she had, but sometimes you just knew.

Karen was looking at her, obviously waiting for an answer, but Laurel had discovered the best thing about everyone thinking you were flaky was you had the luxury of taking time before answering. At last, she simply said, "Yes. I'm seeing him again." And taking him a first edition copy of an old Raymond Chandler novel that she'd found in one of the used bookstores near her place.

No doubt Karen hadn't noticed that Ron had removed his profile from the dating site and she suspected he wouldn't be going on many more first dates. Coffee or otherwise.

"Huh. Well, there's no accounting for tastes, no pun intended." And Laurel was left wondering which of them Karen had just insulted.

"Anyhow," Karen continued, "I think it's time I stepped in and had a little talk with the reluctant groom."

"You called him?" Laurel liked Karen, she really did. It was impossible not to, but she was getting the feeling that the wedding planner was going through a phase of some sort that wasn't entirely conducive to helping Chelsea and David find perfect happiness.

"No. He called me."

"Really? What did he want?"

"I don't know, but he's going to get some advice. If he lets that amazing woman get away because he is too scared of commitment, then he's the biggest fool alive. And that's what I plan to tell him."

Laurel never thought of herself as a brave person. She more liked to stay in the background of life and observe, but she cared about Chelsea and she didn't think she could live with herself if she didn't try to protect her from Marriage's Avenging Angel.

"Are you sure this is about David and Chelsea?"

Karen was such a strong woman, always in control.

But as she met Laurel's gaze, the tough attitude collapsed and her eyes filled with emotion. "You mean, am I interfering in other people's business out of some twisted need of my own? I don't think so. Dex has gone back to New York. I doubt I'll be seeing him again."

"Why? What did he do?"

"He told me he loved me." She seemed for a second as though she might cry, but she pulled herself together. "And I walked away. Now he doesn't send me sexy texts anymore and he's back in New York and I... I just want David to understand that he could lose Chelsea if he doesn't stop being so scared of love and marriage."

"Maybe you should call him."

"But I'm seeing him in half an—"

"Not David. Dexter. Maybe you should call him. I don't know, go for counseling or something. You seemed so happy when he was around."

"I think it's too late. Anyhow, today is about Chelsea and David."

"Are you sure Chelsea would want you to—"

"No! Of course she wouldn't. And I don't want Chelsea to know I interfered. That's why I need you to keep her focused on mushrooms or whatever until I get back. Can I trust you to keep it a secret that I'm seeing her man?"

Laurel called on the universe to shore up her courage. "Only if you promise not to make things worse."

"Of course I won't. David loves her. He probably just needs a gentle nudge." She looked at Laurel and her blue eyes started to dance. "With a cattle prod."

DAVID WAS WAITING for her at the restaurant he'd chosen. It was an Italian restaurant halfway between both their offices and the kind of place where neither of them were likely to bump into anyone they knew.

She felt momentarily guilty at meeting Chelsea's fiancé without her knowledge, but she knew she was doing this for the best so she sucked up her courage and went forward. She'd planned to hug him since she'd met David a few times and he'd always been friendly. But he stuck out his hand in a formal way, so she shook his hand instead. Weird.

When the hostess seated them, he asked for a quiet table in the back of the room and her feeling of subterfuge was heightened.

They made small talk over menus but she wasn't really reading what was listed. It was too tempting. When the waitress came for her order she asked for salad. No dressing.

David, of course, went for a rich pasta dish. No doubt there'd be garlic bread. Garlic bread was one of her weaknesses. Maybe this place wasn't the ritziest Italian restaurant on the planet, but it had all the right scents. Garlic and tomato sauce, rich cream and who knew what else? All she knew was that if she breathed in too deep she'd gain a pound.

She needed to think about something else before she called the young woman with the dyed black hair and the nose stud back and changed her order. "I was surprised to get your call," she said.

"I bet." His brows pulled together. "I wasn't sure I was going to call after the other night."

She reached for a bread stick. Snapped it in half, told herself she'd only nibble. "The other night?"

He had really great eyes, and usually they were full of charm, but right now they seemed pretty chilly. "Do you really think I'm an emotional cripple?"

"No. Of course not. I—"

He was looking at her with skepticism all over his face and suddenly that awful night when she'd forced Chelsea and Laurel out dancing came back to her. "Oh. I texted you, didn't I?"

"Yep."

"Did I really call you an emotion—"

"Yep. I thought the text came from Chels. It was pretty intense."

She put her head in her hands. "Oh, David. I'm so sorry. I can't believe I did that. I was a little…" What was the word she was going for here? Oh, yeah, she knew. Where Dex was concerned, it always came back to the same thing. "Crazy."

"I figured drunk, but okay. It probably turned out to be a good thing, Chelsea and I had a long talk that night."

Her guilt lifted slightly. "Oh, thank heaven. I really wasn't myself that night. I hope you'll forgive me."

His eyes were warming already. He seemed like the kind of man who didn't stay mad for long. There was a twinkle in his baby blues when he said, "For a price."

Putting the bread stick down, she reached for her water. "What kind of price?"

"I think I'm beginning to understand why she doesn't want to get married."

"Well, it's good that you—" She glanced up at him, but he didn't look like he was toying with her. "Did you say *she's* the one who doesn't want to get married?"

"Yep."

"But, I thought—"

"I know you did." He paused here as their food arrived. She was so busy thinking she barely noticed the scent of freshly baked garlic bread wafting over her naked greens like a very bad boy trying to corrupt a determined girl.

When their waitress left, he continued. "Last year I was an ass. I know that now, but when I figured out that I love Chelsea and she's the woman I want to spend my life with, I thought we'd just do it, you know?"

"Get married, you mean?"

"Right. Instead, she's got one excuse after another."

"Chelsea is the one dragging her feet on the wedding?" She felt she needed to clarify this fact once more.

"Yes."

When had she ever been so wrong about anything? Karen always prided herself on being so smart about people. "Wow. I had no idea."

"You want a piece?" He offered her the plate of garlic bread which she'd been eyeing hungrily. She should resist but right now she needed comfort food.

"Sure, thanks."

While she bit into the garlic bread, enjoying it so much she almost moaned, he said, "I'm giving her all the time and space I can because, obviously, I wasn't exactly the most stand-up guy when we were engaged the first time. But that wasn't real. This is real."

He looked so sincere she could see his love for Chelsea shining out of his eyes. *This,* she thought, *this is why I do what I do.* Bringing people together and helping them start their lives together with the most perfect wedding ever.

She leaned forward. "Okay, I was wrong about you. Instead of apologizing again, I'd like you to tell me, what can I do to help?"

"I was hoping you'd say that. Here's the problem.

Chelsea feels like weddings are part of her work life, plus her folks aren't exactly the poster parents for divorced couples with families. Then there are my parents who are so eager for this wedding, it's sort of scary, and everybody at my work wants to be involved. Honestly, I think she's freaked out."

"I can imagine how that could feel."

"The other night, after we talked and I told her how much I wanted to marry her, she suddenly said, 'Okay, let's get married.' But I could tell she was doing it for me."

"David, she loves you, I'm sure of it—"

"Oh, yeah, it's not that. I'm sure she loves me, too. It's the wedding that's making her crazy."

"So, what are you going to do?"

"We're going to elope. And I need your help."

She frowned. "I don't think I've ever planned an elopement."

"I know it probably sounds insane, but I want to surprise her. If I suggest we elope she'll argue with me, she won't want to let down her parents and mine and all our friends and coworkers."

Karen thought about how much she'd been looking forward to planning Chelsea and David's wedding and knew exactly what he was referring to.

"You're right. She will. So what do you need me to do?"

He looked boyishly excited as he pulled out brochures. "Here are three resorts that do weddings. What do you think?"

He shoved them across the table at her. All featured crystal water oceans, beaches, weddings with tropical sunsets pictured in the background. She pushed them all back across the table. "These are all really beautiful, but

I don't know, David. I think she'd want to get married in Paris."

"Paris?"

"Yes."

"But the weather's so crummy there this time of year."

"It's Paris. Who cares?" She glanced up at him. "Anyhow, it's your honeymoon. When are you going to be outside?"

"True. And they do have some incredible hotels there."

"Yep, you could stay at George V or Crillon. Oh, and think of the restaurants. She could eat in all the best places, restaurants she couldn't afford when she was living in Paris and studying." Her enthusiasm built as she thought of all the positive aspects of Paris as an elopement destination. "She could have her good friend give her away, what's his name? The one she met in cooking school."

"Phillipe?"

"That's the one. Then after a few days in Paris maybe you could go somewhere in the Mediterranean. That's what I think she'd like. But, you know, it might be better if you asked her. A wedding is an important part of a woman's life. If you surprise her and get it wrong, her memories will always be a little bit tainted."

He shoved the brochures back into his pocket. "I wish you weren't so right. I'll talk to her. Paris—why didn't I think of that?"

She crunched some salad, still in planning mode. "Maybe we could have a simple reception when you get back? So the parents and friends can still be part of your celebration. I know I'd like that."

"Thanks, Karen. That's a great idea."

He pulled out his BlackBerry and made a notation. Then he glanced up.

"How do you say *I do* in French?"

She and Dexter had talked about going to Paris. Well, doing all of Europe. She'd never been and Dex had promised to show her all the sights. She doubted she'd ever go now.

"Oui," she told David. "Whatever anyone asks you, just say, *Oui."*

24

"Maybe another I-beam," Dex suggested to the construction foreman as they stood contemplating the fact that the Philadelphia hotel's structure had a few weaknesses they were uncovering as the renovation began.

In his experience there were always unforeseen issues in a building this old, but with the wonders of modern technology and building materials, most could be fixed while still maintaining the architectural integrity.

"Yeah. I was thinking the same thing."

"Then we could use some of the reclaimed brick—"

"So you are still in town," a cool female voice hailed him.

He turned. "Sophie? How did you get in here?"

She smiled at him. Nodded to the foreman. "Never doubt the abilities of a tenacious woman."

Since she had a look in her eye that suggested he didn't care to have a bunch of construction guys hear their conversation, he said, "How 'bout I buy you a coffee?"

"Why don't you?"

He gave the foreman a few instructions and then left with Sophie on his arm and a wary feeling in his gut.

She waited until they were out of earshot before saying, "I haven't seen you since Christmas. You don't return calls."

"I'm busy."

"I had my last wedding planning meeting today, and it was weird without you."

He'd known it, of course, since Sophie had e-mailed him the date and texted him and left a phone message. He grabbed his thick coat and held the door for her to exit. "How's Karen?"

"She looks pale. And like she's not getting enough sleep. Sort of like you look. When I walked in for our meeting, she definitely was hoping you'd be there. I could tell she was disappointed you weren't."

"Like I said, I'm busy with work. Besides, the wedding's all planned. You don't need me. Karen's fantastic at what she does."

"I know. I like you both being there, that's all. I'm used to it. And you have good ideas."

He led her into the closest coffee shop and when they were both settled with lattes, he said, "You didn't come here to tell me I missed a meeting. What's up?"

"Honestly, I want to make sure you'll be at the wedding. Andrew's counting on you as his best man. If you're going all high school on me and can't be in the same room with your ex then I need to know about it."

"Of course I'll be there for the wedding. I'm looking forward to it."

"Good."

"Aren't you?"

Sophie shrugged her slender shoulders. "I guess. Mostly I just miss Andrew. I wish he were here."

"I'm sure he feels the same way."

"He does. In fact, he went ahead and booked me a flight to Italy for the week before the wedding."

"Really?"

"Yep. I'll be able to relax and spend some time with the man I love. Then we'll fly home for the wedding. It'll be so much better than hanging around waiting. And this way, I don't spend Valentine's Day on my own. You know?"

"Sure."

She sipped her drink. "She asked after you, by the way."

A flicker of hope stabbed at his chest. "Really."

"Yep. She asked how you were. And she'd really dressed up for the meeting."

"She always dresses well."

"It was a dress designed to get her man back. A woman can tell these things."

He thought this woman was too filled with romantic notions to be a reliable witness, but he appreciated the effort. "All she has to do is call me," he said. He'd been waiting for that call for so many weeks that he knew now it wouldn't come.

He'd been wrong about Karen. She didn't love him enough to battle back her demons. And the loss of her for the second time was more painful than he'd imagined possible.

As bittersweet as it would be to see his ex-wife again, he was all but counting the days.

They finished their coffees and Sophie gave him a big hug as she was leaving. "I'm telling you, she misses you."

He hugged her back. "Have fun in Italy. Tell Andrew hi."

"See you at the wedding."

"SOME DAYS I FEEL like I was put on earth to help people celebrate true love," Karen said to Laurel, in a particularly good mood since the Vanderhooven wedding was today and everything, including the weather, seemed to be smiling on the event.

"Which is weird considering you don't believe in love."

"Yes, I do."

Laurel had changed subtly over the past weeks. Karen couldn't put her finger on what it was, but the woman seemed more outspoken than she used to be. And she had a certain glow about her as though she knew all the secrets of the universe. It was both attractive and, to someone who felt that all the secrets were forever hidden from her, kind of annoying.

The cake creator was working on the finishing touches to Sophie Vanderhooven's cake and it was, perhaps, her greatest achievement yet.

"That is so beautiful," Karen said, pleasure gushing through her. The cake was tiered in traditional style but Laurel had taken the garden theme and made a whimsical, tiered garden, with a twist. It was a Tuscan garden complete with olive trees, lemon trees and cascades of purple bougainvillea, all done in icing.

Just looking at the cake made her happy.

She'd even dressed to match the garden theme in a dark green suit, the color of rose leaves, with a white silk camisole underneath and brand-new shoes to match.

Everything was on track for a wedding that would be as close to perfect as any wedding can be. Of course, she'd have to see Dexter again, but she planned to stay as far in the background as possible and out of his way.

Then, after today, she'd never have to see him again. If the thought brought more pain than she'd imagined, she knew she'd get used to it. Experience had taught her that heartbreak dulled over time.

While she was admiring the cake, and trying to ignore the racket of Chelsea's crew preparing the food that would be served at the reception later, Chelsea came up behind them. There was a sparkle in her eyes and a glow that had nothing to do with cosmetics.

Laurel glanced up, gazed at Chelsea for a few moments and then went back to her task of piping tiny green leaves. "When are you leaving?" she asked.

Chelsea put her hands on her hips and tried to pout. "I thought I was going to surprise you. How did you know David and I are eloping to Paris?"

"Your fiance's not very good at keeping secrets. He's getting us to organize a reception for when you get back."

"Yeah, I wanted to talk to you about that." She tied her white apron tighter around her slim waist. "Who's catering the reception?"

"You are," Karen informed her.

"What?" She looked both horrified and relieved.

"Come on, you know you wouldn't be happy if we got one of your competitors to cater your reception, so we have a plan. Don't we, Laurel?"

"That's right. You pick out what you want and Anton and I will manage your staff. You know Anton can make your recipes almost as good as you can yourself."

"Well, his puff pastry is excellent, but he has a tendency to put too much salt in his sauces. I should—"

"Relax, that's what you should do." Karen took her friend by the shoulders and gave her a little shake. "We all love you. We want to do this for you. After you're back and married and there's no stress."

The women exchanged a quick hug. "Thanks," Chelsea said. Then, as though she couldn't help herself, added, "I'm so happy."

"You should be. You deserve it." Since such sentiments threatened to make both women damp-eyed, Chelsea turned to Laurel and asked, "What kind of cake are you making me?"

"The Eiffel tower."

"Isn't that a little—I don't know. Unlike you? It's so obvious."

Laurel chuckled and adjusted a tiny lemon on a tiny lemon tree. "Sometimes I surprise even myself. But I thought about it and the Eiffel Tower is the perfect metaphor for the relationship between you and David. It's strong and yet elegant, iconic and unforgettable."

"Wow. Thanks."

"I think most people associate the Eiffel tower with romance and Paris, obviously, where you trained and where you're getting married." She bent close to her cake to nudge a purple petal. "I can change it if you want."

"No," Chelsea said. "You are right as always. It is perfect."

"When are you leaving?" Karen asked.

"Whenever you can do without me for a couple of weeks."

"How does Sunday sound?"

She and David had already planned the dates, but she didn't feel any need to share that with Chelsea.

"Really?" she squealed. "You can do without me so fast?"

"It's all arranged."

Chelsea put a hand on her belly and breathed deeply. "I can't believe I'm finally getting married after being engaged twice. To the same man."

"I know," Karen said. "It's so great."

Anton's voice interrupted them. "Chels, can you check this pomegranate infusion? I'm not sure it's thick enough."

The wedding was taking place at the bride's aunt's estate, one of the grand old homes still remaining in the Main Line suburbs.

After checking that everything was running smoothly on the food end, Karen grabbed her binder, her pack of supplies and headed for her car.

She arrived to the usual scene of organized chaos. Flowers were arriving right on schedule, her delivery guys were carrying in stacks of chairs for the ballroom where the actual wedding would take place.

In order to convey the garden theme for a winter wedding, the floral designer, Bertrand, had brought in fresh flowers by the truckload. The effect made her smile. To see pots of daffodils, irises, tulips and hyacinths sending out their evocative fragrance, and tubs of roses arranged in formation to give the idea that the indoor space was a garden of different beds representing different seasons.

The designer was directing the placing of pots of chrysanthemums himself. Even though she'd seen a sketch of the design she was still enthralled by the real thing.

"You have outdone yourself, Bertrand," she cried.

"I think so," he said. Bertrand was not a man who underrated his own talents. He came forward to greet her, an urbane man with a goatee and wearing a black silk blazer, to kiss her on both cheeks. "By holding the ceremony in an ever-blooming garden we suggest that love is always in season."

Trite, perhaps and, given the national divorce rate with a slightly higher than fifty percent chance of being true, she still loved the notion.

"It's gorgeous, better even than I'd imagined."

He nodded, not at all surprised that he'd impressed her yet again. But then with the prices he charged, he should be impressive.

She slipped back into the ballroom after the floral crew had finished, as she always did, checking that everything was perfect.

As she walked among the rows of chairs, adjusting this one, moving a potted plant a half an inch that way, her gaze fell on a pot of yellow roses, very like the ones she'd carried at her own wedding. As she walked forward to touch a soft, creamy yellow petal, she felt an odd peace steal over her.

Love did matter.

Couples every day were brave enough to make a commitment before friends and family, cynics and romantics, and do their best to make a go of it. She took a moment to silently wish Sophie and Andrew success in their married life.

She'd been alone, with two hundred empty chairs and hundreds of blooming plants representing the four seasons, from snowdrops to chrysanthemums and even a tub or two of holly. Suddenly, she knew she wasn't alone anymore. She felt a presence.

Turned.

Dexter was standing before her in his tux, and in that moment she was transported back to her wedding day. They were both older now, but her heart still jumped painfully to see him in that outfit, so reminiscent of the day she'd promised to love him forever, for better or worse.

Trouble was, nobody had explained that the worse might include infidelity. She'd put up with a great deal, but after living with a father who couldn't keep his pants zipped, and a mother who made excuses, she knew she couldn't repeat that pattern.

She forced her racing pulse to slow—and when that didn't work, she hoped he wouldn't notice his effect on her and walked calmly forward.

"Place looks great," he said. His eyes warmed as they looked her over. "And so do you, Kiki. I always liked that color on you."

"Thanks. This is my favorite part," she admitted. "These last few hours when everything's all excitement and coming together into the most perfect wedding."

"Do you ever get tired of it?"

"Never. Every wedding is unique. Every story is theirs to be written."

"Seen the bride yet?"

"No." A tiny frown tried to settle but she wouldn't let it. There was time yet. "She should be here any minute to start getting changed. How 'bout you? Seen the groom?"

"No. I think he's coming straight from the airport."

She shook her head. "I really hate it when people cut the time that fine. What if the plane's late?"

"Relax," he said soothingly, which was easy for him to say when he wasn't the one planning the wedding. "Everything's going to be fine."

"I'm sure you're right."

"I've—" The door opened and he stepped back. She wondered what he'd been going to say. *I've missed you?* It's what she would have said if she had the guts. She'd missed him. Seeing him again only reminded her of how badly.

Sophie's aunt entered the space. "Sorry to interrupt, Karen, but the wedding party seems to be arriving."

"Sophie and Andrew?"

"Not yet. Only the minor royalty so far."

Bridesmaids and groomsmen streamed in the big front doors and Karen sent them to their assigned rooms and still there was no bride or groom. "Where's Sophie?" she asked the maid of honor.

"She's coming in with Andrew, I think."

"You mean she's picking him up at the airport? I specifically told her to—"

"No. She's there. With him. In Italy. They're coming in on the same plane."

"But—" There was no point telling the poor maid of honor that the bride wasn't following agreed-on protocol. "Never mind," she said with her reassuring smile. "They've got plenty of time."

She was slightly less reassured when the guests began arriving. Sophie's aunt sent her increasingly questioning glances and she could only reply with an uplifting of the shoulders. She had no idea where the bride was. Sophie wasn't answering her cell phone nor the groom his.

To get away from the melee, Karen walked into the kitchen where Chelsea was overseeing food and drink and David was serving as a bartender as he sometimes did in order to be with his fiancée on a big night.

He was exuberant and surprised Karen by picking her up and swinging her in a circle. "I got her to commit. Did you see that?"

She laughed. "I did."

He was so happy it was impossible not to laugh. "Oh, David," Chelsea said, her apron covering one of her designer Paris dresses. "Stop goofing around and slice lemons or something useful."

"Henpecked already," he complained, before heading off to do as he was bid.

"Coming through," Laurel's voice could be heard, louder and more commanding than usual.

Laurel was bringing in her cake. This was always a tense time for her as one slip and fall meant that days of hard work were lost and the wedding would be minus one cake. To Karen's surprise, Ron was with her, helping. "Ron, hi," she said, surprised.

"Hello, Karen," he said, as though he was to be found in the back kitchen of all her weddings. Whatever, she had no time to visit.

"Okay, I've got the table all set up ready for the cake. Follow me." She cleared the way and between them they got the cake safely stowed in the large formal dining room. Laurel fussed with it a bit until the confectionary garden was once again perfect.

Ron stepped back to watch Laurel, and she bet he didn't even realize he was smiling like a lovestruck fool.

He was dressed as neatly as always but somehow he appeared more casual. She guessed it was because his entire attitude was so much more relaxed.

And then it hit her like a bolt of lightning. There were only the three of them in the large room. She said, "Ron, would you mind going into the kitchen and bringing me a pair of scissors?"

"I'd be happy to," he said, and left.

"What do you need scissors for?" Laurel asked.

She waited until he was out of the room. "I don't. I wanted to get you alone." It all made sense now, the way Laurel had been so different lately, the glow about her. "You're sleeping with him, aren't you?"

Laurel opened her mouth to reply but it was Chelsea who answered. She'd arrived in time to hear Karen's last words. "Have you just figured that out?" She sounded pretty amused.

"I—I've had other things on my mind. Usually I notice."

"Actually," Laurel said in her soft, diffident way, "he asked me to marry him."

"What?" both women shrieked in unison.

And Laurel—quiet, flaky Laurel—laughed aloud, pulling them both in for a hug. "I never would have met him if it wasn't for you two. I am so happy."

"But it's so fast."

"I know. Honestly, I think I knew the second I saw him."

"Love at first sight. Huh. So it really can happen."

Chelsea nodded. "Happened to me, the first time I saw David. Of course, I was only fourteen at the time and he didn't know I was alive. But I didn't care. I loved him anyway."

At that moment Dexter walked in. Karen looked across the room at him, recalled the first day they'd met, and how she'd taken one look at him and felt as though time had stopped and the world stilled.

"It happened to me, too," she admitted.

25

"WHAT HAPPENED TO YOU, too?" Dex asked.

She ignored his question. "Tell me you have news?"

"I was hoping you'd have some."

She shook her head. "If only the happy couple would show up, this would be a fantastic wedding."

"Don't panic until you have to," Chelsea advised. Her brown eyes were full of sympathy. It was great having a friend like Chelsea. She knew Karen wouldn't worry if there wasn't anything to worry about. "Some things we can't control."

For some reason, they both glanced at Dexter.

Could Chelsea be as aware as she was that where her ex was concerned, she had no control. Not over her feelings, her actions or her heart.

She loved him now, had loved him when she first set eyes on him, would always love him.

"The guests are arriving," Dexter informed her.

But she already knew that. They, at least, were on time.

"I know." There had been no plan for a before

ceremony mingle. This was like a church wedding. Arrive, sit down, ceremony and then reception. The harpist had already started. She could hear the soft strains of music coming from the ballroom.

This had never happened to her before.

Never.

As they stared at each other, twin cell phones began to ring. She reached immediately for hers, saw Dexter do the same.

"It's an incoming text," she said as Laurel and Chelsea watched. As though drawn by some invisible force, David and Ron came into the dining room just as Karen faced her worse nightmare.

"Stuck in Italy," she read aloud. "No way to get back in time. We're going to get married here. We've paid for the wedding so tell everyone to enjoy a great party on us. Sophie."

"My message is shorter but pretty much says the same," Dex added.

KAREN MADE A SOUND she didn't think had ever come out of her mouth before. Could you yell, moan and hyperventilate all at one time? With a little scream thrown in for good measure?

"There's not going to be a wedding," Chelsea said.

Dexter was the only person in the room who didn't seem at all shocked, instead he chuckled. "Good for them," he said.

Finding an outlet for the torrent of emotions swamping her nervous system, Karen swung on him. "Good for them? What are you talking about? I planned a wedding around a bride and groom."

But Dexter simply looked at her for a long moment, a slow smile spreading across his face. How he could be happy in this time of her worst professional humiliation, she couldn't even imagine.

"And all those people out there have traveled a long way to enjoy a wedding," Dexter said. He glanced around, spotted a bouquet of cut flowers on a side table, broke off a yellow rosebud and began stuffing it into his top buttonhole. "They gave up their Saturdays, got dressed up."

Chelsea regarded him with interest. "Yes, they have, it would be a real shame to disappoint them," she agreed.

"I'll have to tell them," Karen said, feeling stunned and stupid. And why, oh why was Dex sticking flowers in his lapel at a time like this?

Laurel, who'd quietly watched Dex, seemed to have caught the bug and she'd abandoned her cake to choose a selection of blooms from the bouquet. "I need a kitchen towel," she said urgently to Chelsea. "And some ribbon. Do we have anything in green?"

"What are you lunatics doing?" Karen demanded.

Dex walked forward, laughter deep in his eyes, and an emotion so strong it made her pulse pound in spite of the fact that she had really important things to do here. He reached for her hands.

"I love you, Karen. In front of all these witnesses, I swear to you that I have always loved you. I never was unfaithful to you, never could be. You're my muse, my insanity, the thorn in my side and the woman I dream about at night and want to wake up to every morning."

He laughed as her mouth opened and closed a few times but nothing came out.

"Come on, Kiki. Accept the truth. You let your insecurities get in the way of the best thing that ever happened to either of us. What say you give us another chance?"

"But, I can't just—"

"Seems to me," Chelsea said, helping Laurel tie her makeshift bouquet, "that a good wedding planner should be prepared for every eventuality, including supplying a bride and groom if the original pair go missing."

"But I—"

"What, Kiki? You what?" Dexter was still holding her hands, still looking at her with his heart in his eyes and she knew.

Crazy, with no way to prove anything, she knew.

"Oh, Dex, are you sure?"

"I'm game if you are."

Strains of harp music penetrated the dining room as the door opened and Sophie's aunt came in looking as distracted as a seventy-year-old society matron can look. "The guests appear to be getting restless," she said.

Chelsea moved to the woman to speak to her quietly since Karen only had eyes for Dexter. "But I'm impossible. I'm jealous and neurotic and a perfectionist."

"I know."

"And I'll never get any taller. And probably not a lot thinner. I'll probably gobble up that entire cake and get fat."

"I love you exactly the way you are."

Tears filled her eyes. "Do you, Dex? Do you really?"

Instead of answering her with words, he leaned in and kissed her with passion and warmth. Felt like all the answer she needed.

She nodded, decision made.

Then, as everyone in the room was looking at her, she did what she did best. Planned a wedding.

"Chelsea? I'll need you to be my maid of honor."

"I'm touched and I accept." Chelsea removed her apron and looked as chic as any bridesmaid could in her Paris gown.

"Best man?" Dex asked David.

"Happy to help. I'm David by the way." The men shook hands.

"But who's going to walk me down the aisle?"

Ron stepped forward. "I would be honored, as a friend who thinks the world of you, to walk you down the aisle."

"But Laurel? You'll have to be a bridesmaid. I can't leave Laurel out."

"I'm not really dressed for it." They all looked at her in one of her usual flowing numbers and Karen thought she'd never looked better.

"You're perfect."

"What would you like me to do?" the aunt asked, seeming much less hysterical about this change of plans than Karen would have imagined.

"Perhaps you could make an announcement," Dex said. "If you're up to it."

"I suppose it's no more complicated than speaking to the Ladies' Auxiliary," she informed him tartly.

"Then let's go."

He held her hand tightly and they walked to the double doors that led to the conservatory.

Sophie's aunt opened the door and two hundred faces turned to look. Some were bored, some irritated and some simply enjoying the music and the day.

Dexter spoke to her in a low voice and she repeated

the words, putting her own spin on them, naturally, to the rather stunned looking congregation.

"Dear friends," she said, every inch the grand lady. "I've got some rather surprising news for you. My niece and her fiancé were unable to fly back from Italy in time for today's ceremony."

There were a few startled cries and an immediate rustle of comment and shuffling. But a congregation of two hundred restless and confused wedding-goers were no match for a woman who'd been a top society matron for decades. She simply raised her voice.

"I know it's unfortunate, but I promised you a wedding in this house today, and a wedding you shall have."

She waited another moment for the latest batch of murmurs to die down. "Many of you know Dexter Crane, if not personally, then by reputation. He's a dear friend of the family and I'm delighted to help him celebrate his wedding to Philadelphia's favorite wedding planner, Karen Petersham, whom many of you know personally or certainly by reputation.

"Karen and Dexter would like your support and congratulations as they celebrate their marriage here, today."

"Rings," Chelsea whispered urgently. "You don't have rings."

Karen had never been more glad that she always had emergency supplies. She slipped off the gold band she always wore on these occasions, kissed it quickly for good luck, then passed it to David, Dexter slipped off the signet ring he always wore and followed her lead, kissing it quickly before passing that to David.

The aunt took one look at the homemade bouquet and shook her head. She walked over to where a gaggle of confused young women in blue bridesmaid dresses stood and took the bridal bouquet from the maid of honor and handed it to Karen. "Something borrowed."

She then took the heirloom pearls from her own neck and looped them around Karen's. Who was so surprised she blinked. The older woman's eyes crinkled when she smiled. "I wore these on my wedding day. They've been worn by all the brides in my family, and we've all enjoyed very long, successful marriages."

Karen glanced at Dex in panic, then back at the woman. "But Dex and I were married before and it didn't work out."

"Well, whatever foolish mistakes you made before, don't make them again," she told Karen quite forcibly. Then she surveyed her once more. "Right, that's something old, something borrowed, your clothing's obviously new. That just leaves something blue."

"I'm actually wearing blue underwear," Karen said, feeling a little foolish.

"Excellent foresight." The woman nodded briskly. "Now who is going to walk you down the aisle?"

"I've offered, ma'am," Ron informed her.

"Good. Now," she motioned to Dex and David, "you two skedaddle up to the front, then I'll take my seat and motion to the harp to begin. Oh, and you'd better give the minister your full names so he doesn't muff it up." Then she beamed at them both. "Good luck, my dears."

It was perhaps the oddest wedding party Karen had ever been a part of. Six confused young women in designer blue bridesmaid gowns trooped up the makeshift aisle, followed by Laurel and Chelsea both stylish in their own ways, but very different from the other attendants. Then Karen followed on Ron's arm, in her green suit and the most glorious bouquet of flowers. The pearls were warm around her neck, warm with tradition and generations of successful brides.

She wouldn't have worn them if she'd thought she'd break the tradition, but she knew she wouldn't. She and Dex had broken faith with each other once. They wouldn't do it again.

Of that she was certain.

When she walked down the aisle, before a congregation of people who seemed as delighted to celebrate her wedding as they would have been to celebrate Sophie's, she felt a connection with all the women who'd dared to believe in love, dared to make a commitment.

Her gaze rose and she met Dex's, his eyes so warm and full of promise.

And love.

"Dearly beloved," the minister began and she looked at Dexter and thought how dearly beloved he was to her.

The service, so unexpected, so perfect, could have been designed with them in mind. Then she realized that Sophie had pretty much left it to Dex and Karen to plan her wedding.

No wonder they'd planned the perfect wedding for themselves.

When the minister said, "You may kiss the bride," Dexter took her in his arms and kissed her, managing to be both decorous and passionate. As he pulled away, he held her for a moment.

"We'll do better, this time, Kiki."

"We'll do better, Dex," she promised. "We will."

* * * * *

HARLEQUIN® Blaze™

COMING NEXT MONTH

Available October 26, 2010

#573 THE REAL DEAL
Lose Yourself...
Debbi Rawlins

#574 PRIVATE AFFAIRS
Private Scandals
Tori Carrington

#575 NORTHERN ENCOUNTER
Alaskan Heat
Jennifer LaBrecque

#576 TAKING CARE OF BUSINESS
Forbidden Fantasies
Kathy Lyons

#577 ONE WINTER'S NIGHT
Encounters
Lori Borrill

#578 TOUCH AND GO
Michelle Rowen

REQUEST YOUR FREE BOOKS!

2 FREE NOVELS
PLUS 2
FREE GIFTS!

HARLEQUIN®

Blaze™

Red-hot reads!

YES! Please send me 2 FREE Harlequin® Blaze™ novels and my 2 FREE gifts (gifts are worth about $10). After receiving them, if I don't wish to receive any more books, I can return the shipping statement marked "cancel." If I don't cancel, I will receive 6 brand-new novels every month and be billed just $4.24 per book in the U.S. or $4.71 per book in Canada. That's a saving of at least 15% off the cover price. It's quite a bargain. Shipping and handling is just 50¢ per book.* I understand that accepting the 2 free books and gifts places me under no obligation to buy anything. I can always return a shipment and cancel at any time. Even if I never buy another book, the two free books and gifts are mine to keep forever.

151/351 HDN E5LS

Name _____ (PLEASE PRINT)

Address _____ Apt. #

City _____ State/Prov. _____ Zip/Postal Code

Signature (if under 18, a parent or guardian must sign)

Mail to the **Harlequin Reader Service:**
IN U.S.A.: P.O. Box 1867, Buffalo, NY 14240-1867
IN CANADA: P.O. Box 609, Fort Erie, Ontario L2A 5X3

Not valid for current subscribers to Harlequin Blaze books.

Want to try two free books from another line?
Call 1-800-873-8635 or visit www.morefreebooks.com.

* Terms and prices subject to change without notice. Prices do not include applicable taxes. N.Y. residents add applicable sales tax. Canadian residents will be charged applicable provincial taxes and GST. Offer not valid in Quebec. This offer is limited to one order per household. All orders subject to approval. Credit or debit balances in a customer's account(s) may be offset by any other outstanding balance owed by or to the customer. Please allow 4 to 6 weeks for delivery. Offer available while quantities last.

Your Privacy: Harlequin Books is committed to protecting your privacy. Our Privacy Policy is available online at www.eHarlequin.com or upon request from the Reader Service. From time to time we make our lists of customers available to reputable third parties who may have a product or service of interest to you. If you would prefer we not share your name and address, please check here. ☐

Help us get it right—We strive for accurate, respectful and relevant communications. To clarify or modify your communication preferences, visit us at www.ReaderService.com/consumerchoice.

HB10R

HARLEQUIN®

A Romance

FOR EVERY MOOD™

Spotlight on

Inspirational

Wholesome romances
that touch the heart and soul.

See the next page
to enjoy a sneak peek from
the Love Inspired® Suspense
inspirational series.

See below for a sneak peek from
our inspirational line, Love Inspired® Suspense

Enjoy this heart-stopping excerpt from
RUNNING BLIND
by top author Shirlee McCoy,
available November 2010!

The mission trip to Mexico was supposed to be an
adventure. But the thrill turns sour when Jenna Dougherty
and her roommate Magdalena are kidnapped.

"It's okay. I'm here to help." The voice was as deep as the darkness, but Jenna Dougherty didn't believe the lie. She could do nothing but lie still as hands slid down her arms, felt the rope around her wrists.

"I'm going to use a knife to cut you free, Jenna. Hold still."

The cold blade of a knife pressed close to her head before her gag fell away.

"I—" she started, but her mouth was dry, and she could do nothing but suck in air.

"Shhh. Whatever needs to be said can be said when we're out of here." Nick spoke quietly, his hand gentle on her cheek. There and gone as he sliced through the ropes on her wrists and ankles.

He pulled her upright. "Come on. We may be on borrowed time."

"I can't leave my friend," Jenna rasped out.

"There's no one here. Just us."

"She has to be here." Jenna took a step away.

"There's no one here. Let's go before that changes."

"It's dark. Maybe if we find a light…"

"What did you say?"

"We need to turn on the light. I can't leave until I know that—"

"What can you see, Jenna?"

"Nothing."

"No shadows? No light?"

"No."

"It's broad daylight. There's light spilling in from the window I climbed in through. You can't see it?"

She went cold at his words.

"I can't see anything."

"You've got a nasty bruise on your forehead. Maybe that has something to do with it." His fingers traced the tender flesh on her forehead.

"It doesn't matter *how* it happened. I'm blind!"

Can Nick help Jenna find her friend or will chasing this trail have Jenna running blindly again into danger?

Find out in RUNNING BLIND, available in November 2010 only from Love Inspired Suspense.

FROM #1 *NEW YORK TIMES*
AND *USA TODAY* BESTSELLING AUTHOR

DEBBIE MACOMBER

Mrs. Miracle on 34th Street…

This Christmas, Emily Merkle (just call her Mrs. Miracle)
is working in the toy department at Finley's, the last
family-owned department store in Manhattan.

Her boss (who happens to be the owner's son) has placed
an order for a large number of high-priced robots, which
he hopes will give the business a much-needed boost. In
fact, Jake Finley's counting on it.

Holly Larson is counting on that robot, too. She's been
looking after her eight-year-old nephew, Gabe, ever since
her widowed brother was deployed overseas. Holly plans
to buy Gabe a robot—which she can't afford—because
she's determined to make Christmas special.

But this Christmas will be different—thanks to Mrs.
Miracle. Next to bringing children joy, her favorite activity
is giving romance a nudge. Fortunately, Jake and Holly
are receptive to her "hints." And thanks to Mrs. Miracle,
Christmas takes on new meaning for Jake. For all of them!

Call Me Mrs. Miracle

Available wherever books are sold
September 28!

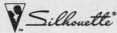

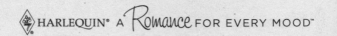

"I didn't mean to spend the night,"
Dex said

"I didn't mean to let you." This was all too intimate, too familiar. In a minute, he'd suggest they shower together, or she would, and then they'd drink coffee and share the paper. She'd kiss him goodbye and wish him a good day.

"I'd almost forgotten how good we are together," he murmured.

The memories of the night before made Karen smile with pleasure mixed with mild embarrassment. She'd been like a sex-crazed maniac. "I'll never look at Chinese food the same way."

He nuzzled her ear. "You still taste like plum sauce. We should take a shower together."

Yep, right on cue. As though they were still the happily married couple who had sex with their takeout and showered together in the morning.

If they were so good together, why weren't they still married?

Dear Reader,

I'm a huge fan of old movies. I can't get enough of them, especially the romantic comedies. I clearly had *The Philadelphia Story* in mind when I wrote *The Ex Factor* and if I got stuck, I'd think to myself, What would Cary Grant do? What would Katharine Hepburn do? And then I'd know.

This book features some of the characters I wrote about in my previous Harlequin Blaze title *My Fake Fiancée* (July 2010), so if you want to read Chelsea and David's story, that's where you'll want to go for that.

Thanks, as always, for coming along with me on these wonderful adventures. I always have fun writing them. Visit me on the Web at www.nancywarren.net.

Happy reading,

Nancy Warren